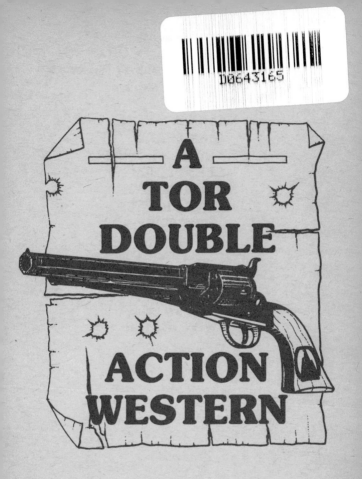

A
TOR
DOUBLE

ACTION
WESTERN

Look for Tor Double Action Westerns
from these authors

FRANK BONHAM
MAX BRAND
HARRY SINCLAIR DRAGO
CLAY FISHER
NORMAN A. FOX
STEVE FRAZEE
ZANE GREY
WILL HENRY
WAYNE D. OVERHOLSER
LEWIS B. PATTEN
JOHN PRESCOTT
W. C. TUTTLE
OWEN WISTER

Max Brand

RANGE JESTER
BLACK THUNDER

TOR

A TOM DOHERTY ASSOCIATES BOOK
NEW YORK

RANGE JESTER

Copyright © 1932 by Street & Smith Publications, Inc.
Copyright renewed © 1960 by Dorothy Faust. First appeared in *Western Story Magazine*.

BLACK THUNDER

Copyright © 1933 by Popular Publications, Inc.
Copyright renewed © 1961 by Dorothy Faust. First appeared in *Dime Western*.

A Tor Book
Published by Tom Doherty Associates, Inc.
49 West 24th Street
New York, N.Y. 10010

Cover art by Faba

ISBN: 0-812-51618-4

First edition: July 1991

Printed in the United States of America

0 9 8 7 6 5 4 3 2 1

RANGE JESTER

CHAPTER 1
Horizon Trails

THREE MEN CAME OVER THE HORIZON. THE FIRST CAME through the pass; the second, up the valley; the third walked in over the flats from the direction of the railroad. All three were headed for Loomis and one of them was to die before morning.

The man in the pass was Rance Tucker, flogging a pair of little mustangs in front of his buckboard, which jumped and danced over the stones and the icy ruts of that trail. As he drove, he leaned forward in his seat a little, as though even that slight inclination of the body got him a vital degree closer to his necessary goal.

He was a big man in his early forties, rawboned, with a weather-beaten face and a great crag of a jaw. As he came out of the mouth of the pass, he first looked apprehensively behind him, for he thought that he had heard the pattering hoofs of a horse galloping through the ravine. But that might well be in his mind; for days a dread had been gathering in him.

When he saw the iron-colored walls of the ravine behind him and nothing living between them, he flogged the mustangs again, until they humped their hindquarters, switched their tails and shook their heads in protest. But, according to the ways of their kind, they only lurched for an instant into a rapid lope, and then fell back to the dogtrot which was all they knew about a road gait.

Tucker forgot to whip them for a moment and stared down through the gloom of the winter evening into Loomis Valley. It was a heavy dusk, for the sky was sheeted across with gray, and long arms of shadow reached out of the heavens toward the earth, covering the mountains, obscuring utterly the level reaches of the desert, thronging over the lower end of the valley itself. There was the brittle chill of frost in the air, and before morning probably the ground would be covered with white. But the darkness only served to make the lights of Loomis shine more clearly, a little bright cluster in the middle of the valley.

Rance Tucker sighed and nodded with reassurance as he made out the spot. He could remember when this had been Parker Valley, and yonder stood the town of Parkerville. But Parkerville had burned to the ground, and when the ashes were hardly cold, before they had had a chance to blow away, in fact, Dave Loomis came along and bought up the entire site for next to nothing. It was only a crossroads little town, at the best, but Loomis built his hotel there, installing a blacksmith shop in a wing of it. He also found room for a post office and a general merchandise store. What more does a town need, except a barroom, which the hotel offered, and some sort of a dining room, which the same hotel possessed, of course? So the hotel stood in place of the vanished town of Parkerville and everybody was satisfied, particularly Dave Loomis!

That hotel was the goal of Rance Tucker. He

had barely settled himself back in his seat and commenced clucking again to his horses, however, when he heard the sound of hoofs again behind him, and this time unmistakably.

He looked back with eyes that started from his head. Like a ghost appeared the rider in the gloaming, but Rance Tucker, with a groan of fear, jerked the horses to a stand, pulled a double-barreled shotgun loaded with buckshot from beneath the seat and, dropping low down, leveled his weapon, blinking rapidly to clear his eyes of the tears which the wind had brought there.

The rider came swiftly on, saw the gleam of the leveled gun, and jumped his horse far to the side with a yell:

"Hey, Dad!"

Rance Tucker got up from his knees with a groan of relief. His big body began to tremble with weakness, now that the strain upon him was relaxed.

"Hey, you, Lew," he answered, rather feebly. "Whatcha mean by coming out like this? Your place is back there at home."

Lew Tucker reined his horse in beside the buckboard and scowled at his father.

He was a huge man, only twenty-two, but already seasoned and hard; his strength was in full maturity as often happens when boys lead a life of constant activity.

"Lookit here, Dad," he said. "It's all right you telling me to stay at home, but Ma wouldn't have me there."

"Whatcha mean? Wouldn't have you there?" shouted the father, relieving himself by falling into a rage.

"That's what I mean," said the young man. "You don't think that you been pulling the wool over the eyes of anybody, the way you been acting for a couple weeks, do you?"

"Acting how?" asked Rance Tucker, with a little less vehemence.

"Acting," said Lew Tucker, "as though there was Injuns lyin' in wait in the next room at home or over the hill, when you're out riding. And staying up all last night, walking up and down; that's not deceivin' anybody, is it? There's certainly something on your mind, and you're drivin' to Loomis to get it off!"

This assemblage of facts broke down the self-assurance of the older man.

He said: "Look, Lew, you know that Barry Home is comin' back tonight, don't you? Tonight or tomorrow, he's sure gonna turn up, and who would wanta be alone on a ranch when that murdering devil comes back?"

"How d'you mean, alone?" asked the son. "Ain't you got me as well as yourself? Ain't there two hired men? Ain't four men enough to handle even Barry Home?"

"You think so, do you?" asked the father, gravely.

"Four to one?" repeated Lew Tucker, as though the phrase was a sufficient answer.

"I got a wife and a son, and I got a ranch that I've made out of nothing with my own hands," began Tucker.

"Aw, wait. Don't go through all that again," pleaded Lew Tucker, insolently. "I know all you done, and how poor you and Ma were when you started the climb. Now, you tell me what you're gonna do in Loomis. Go and lie under a bed and shake for a coupla days, waiting for Barry Home to show up? Is that it?"

"Don't sass me back like that," commanded the father. "You think that you're a big, bold, rough feller, you do. But you don't know what Barry Home can do when he gets started!"

"Well, and what could he do?" asked Lew

Tucker. "He ain't more'n half my size, scarcely, and he ain't much older than me, only three or four years. And he's a damn jailbird, besides!"

"He's a jailbird," said the father. "And that means that he's gonna try to work out his grudge agin' me. He swore that he would be even with me when the jury found him guilty. The judge and the jury, they all heard him!"

"What I mean," said the son, "did you do dirt to Barry Home that time? Did you hide the stuff in his room, like he swears that you done? Did you plant it there to get him pinched instead of you?"

"Lew, Lew, what you talkin' about?" exclaimed Rance Tucker.

"I'm askin' you a question."

"And you a son of mine!"

"I ain't saying that I'll let you down. No matter what you've done, you're my father, I reckon, and I'm behind you as long as they's any blood in me. Only, I'd like to know the truth."

"Was you in the courtroom when I give in my evidence?" asked the father.

"It was three year back," said the son, "but I reckon that I could say every word over. Was it true?"

"Did I take an oath on a book before I talked that day?" asked the rancher.

"I reckon that you did."

"Is that enough for you?"

"Yeah, I guess that's gotta be enough, if you put it that way."

"Then go on home with you."

"I won't go home," insisted the son. "I wouldn't dare to. Ma sent me out to have an eye on you, and I'm gonna keep with you till hell freezes over!"

Rance Tucker made a sound of vague discomfort and annoyance deep in his throat and struck his horses with the long whip. They jerked away into the dusk, with a clattering of the ironshod wheels, and young Lew Tucker rode rapidly behind.

Up the lower part of the valley, which was still called "Parker," as distinguished from "Loomis," came another rider at this same time, as tall a man as either of the Tuckers, but with an air about him that suggested a foreign gentility. He was mounted on a horse of such obvious value that all the Tucker mustangs, their saddles, buckboard, harness, and guns together, would not have made half the value of that magnificent stallion.

The rider, taking the wind in his face as he came to the junction of Loomis and Parker valleys, paused to adjust the silken scarf that he wore, in place of a bandanna about his throat. As he paused, the wind turned up the wide brim of his sombrero, though it was stiffened and weighted with Mexican goldwork, and showed for a moment a thin, sallow, handsome face, puckered a bit about the lips as though in great weariness, but with a reserve of fire gleaming in the eyes.

That was Tom London, known far and wide throughout the country, suspected of being a little light in his fingers and lighter still in his conscience. For he was a gentleman without visible means of support, but one, nevertheless, who was constantly able to do as he pleased. Moreover, nothing but the most expensive ever satisfied him. Some said that he was able to make all of his expenses out of gambling, but others shook their heads. Though Tom London was a gentleman who gambled for high stakes, he seemed to lose even more than he won. There must be other sources of his revenue, and what could they be?

However, the question went no further than surmises, for Tom London was the very last person in the world of whom one would wish to ask questions, at least, questions about himself. At the same time, his manner was the most amiable in the world, unless one crossed him suddenly, unexpectedly, and then danger peered out from beneath the straight, black brows.

He finished adjusting his neck cloth and rode on, just as Barry Home, walking through the desert sand, came within sight of the distant glitter of the lights of Loomis and paused in his turn to make a cigarette, light it with his back to the wind, and smoke it out while he remained thinking things over.

CHAPTER 2
Jester of the Range

It IS NOT THE EASIEST THING IN THE WORLD TO MAKE a cigarette in the semidark; it is nearly impossible when a strong wind is blowing. Yet, Barry Home managed the thing with the most consummate ease, never glancing down at what his fingers were accomplishing. Neither did he have any difficulty in lighting the match, holding it for a moment in the secure round cup of his hands, and then opening the thumbs to get the cigarette in contact with the flame.

In this flash one could see his face. It was not the face that Loomis would expect to see. He had gone away as the buffoon, the good-natured jester of the entire range, and he was coming back with the roundness chipped away from his face. In fact, he seemed to be carved in a very different sort of stone!

He was the sort of man who would be described with difficulty. He had blue-gray, sometimes greenish eyes; his hair was ordinary brown; his height was only a shade above average; his weight was about average; there were no marks or scars on his face or on his body. In fact, the whole man could be summed up as "average."

However, though Loomis would have been willing to admit that Barry Home was average in appearance, the community, of which the hotel town was the center, would have been the first to declare that there was nothing average about his mental equipment.

For that matter, when had there been a Home who was simply average?

The grandfather of Barry had been one of those fellows who play the real Indian game. That is to say, you tag the Indians while the Indians are trying to tag you. You do the tagging with the point of a knife, or an ounce of lead placed in a vital spot. And grandfather Home had done a great deal of tagging before the Indians finally put an end to the game and him.

His three sons scattered to different parts of the West. One of them became a booster of small towns and was wiped out in the fire that removed one of these towns from the map.

Another started a gambling palace in Tucson and was said to have run it fairly and squarely. Nevertheless, an irate customer, whose roulette luck had been worse than his fortune in the mines, pulled a sawed-off shotgun from under his coat on a day, and emptied both barrels of it into Home.

That left Barry Home, the third, the sole heir of the family name and the family fortune. The name was a wild one and the fortune was nil.

Barry Home himself seemed to care nothing for the past and nothing for the future. He was content to ride the range, working here and there, a very good hand with cows, a better hand with horses. He was never offensive. His spirits were always high. Some people continually waited for him to show a spark of the old Home fire, but it never appeared, except in his jovial moments. The result was that half the range said that the old blood was burned out at last; the other half said that Barry Home, the third, was the best of the whole wild family.

Then came the day when the Crystal River stage was robbed of sixty odd thousand dollars in hard cash and jewels, following which the trail of a rider from the point of the holdup was traced back to the Tucker ranch.

The print of that horse was oddly like that of one belonging to Tom London. Tom was actually arrested, when suddenly Rance Tucker appeared and reluctantly confessed that he had seen his hired man, Barry Home, returning late on the guilty night, riding a horse whose shoes, in fact, were ringers for those worn by Tom London's thoroughbred.

The sheriff jogged out to the Tucker place and searched the room of Barry Home. He did not find much, only three gold watches and a single batch of currency. But what does a cowpuncher need with three gold watches, when he's working for fifty a month, or less, according to the season?

No one could tell, particularly the judge and the jury that heard the case, and Barry Home was sent to prison, but for only five years, though that State was hard on stage robbers. However, the boy was young; it was a first offense and, though he was threatened with a much longer term unless he would confess where the rest of the loot was hidden, it was a matter of record that he would not budge from his first story of innocence and complete ignorance of how the loot could have appeared in his bedroom at the Tucker ranchhouse. Nevertheless, he was given only five years by the judge, in spite of a furiously ranting district attorney.

Good behavior in the prison, the special intercession of the warden, commuted the five years to three; and now he was out in the world again, a free man.

He had the clothes he stood up in. He had a dollar and sixty-five cents in his pocket. Otherwise, he had one handkerchief, and that was all.

The young man, however, was optimistic. After he had stood there for some time, smoking out the cigarette, and considering the distant gleam of the lights of Loomis, he dropped the butt on the ground, stepped on it, watched the little red shower of sparks blow away, and then stepped forward again, singing.

The angry wind tore the music from his lips and scattered it abroad, as it were; but Barry Home, undaunted, continued to sing. And his step was as light as a dancer's. As he came closer to the long double row of trees that led up to Loomis, he stopped and looked curiously up at their nakedness, barely visible in the rapidly gathering night.

He was, like them, stripped of everything.

They had lived twenty-five years in the world and so had he. Now they had come to a cold, naked winter. So had he.

They were unregarded by the world in the time of their need. And thus it was with him.

When he had come to the conclusion of these somber thoughts, he broke out into contented laughter and walked on again. It was plain that he was as good-natured as ever, and yet it was also plain that that cheerful nature had been changed a little during the three years he had spent away from Loomis and the range around it.

He reached the hotel. First, he stepped onto the front veranda, walked down the length of it, looked at the darkened windows of the store and post office, at the lighted ones of the lobby and sitting room; then turned back and regarded the pale gleam of the water in the troughs that hospitably bordered the whole length of the porch. Something made him dip a finger in that water. The cold of it bit his finger to the bone.

He stepped from the veranda, rounded the hotel, and a great mongrel dog came running toward him, barking furiously out of the night.

"Hello, Tiger, you old bluff!" said the younger man, pleasantly.

Tiger began to whine and sniff at the shoes of the stranger. He did not know the voice, to be sure, but he understood the familiar tone of one who feels that he is at home. Tiger was in a quandary. He began to growl again, when he saw this man walk up to the kitchen door and pull it open.

A thin drift of smoke and of fragrant steam blew out into the night. The young man stepped inside.

He saw Mrs. Dave Loomis, Gertie to the entire range, standing over the big stove in the corner, just now lifting the iron lid of a pot and, with a dripping spoon in one hand, peering through clouds of steam at the contents.

"Hello, Mrs. Loomis," he said, with a smile.

"Hey! Hullo, there, Barry!" she cried.

She gave the metal spoon a fling into the sink, where it arrived with a great clattering. Then she bore down hugely upon the other and held out both hands, red and wet as they were.

"Barry Home!" she cried. "Now, I'm mighty glad to be seeing you, and since when have you started in calling me 'Mrs. Loomis,' I'm asking you. Maybe I'm that old, but I don't want to feel it!"

"Old?" said he, taking the moist hands with a hearty grip. "You're not old. You're just the right age, I think. But I've been taking lessons in politeness for three years, you know. I've learned to use names with a lot of care, I can tell you!"

He laughed, his eyes shining with wonderful

brightness and merriment. Mrs. Loomis sighed with relief, and nodded and smiled in return.

"Barry," she said, "I was thinking that maybe they'd put the iron into you, like they often do. There was that poor fellow Phil Dunlop, you knew him?"

"The killer?"

"Oh, he wasn't no killer in the beginning," said Mr. Loomis. "All he did was to pick up a cow, now and then, just a wanderin' cow or a calf that didn't know where to go, and how could you be blaming a poor fellow with not much of a home except of his own making? He never touched another man's horse! But they got hold of him, and they shipped him away to jail. When he came out, the spirit inside of him had changed, and he was mean. He was a nice boy, when he went away, but he was a gunman when he come back home. But you, Barry, they didn't do nothing to you. Not a thing! Except you're three years older. That's all. And I'm glad. I'm mighty glad. Hey, Patty, come here and look at Barry Home come back to us! And just the same as ever he was in the old days!"

The girl came out of the pantry with a bread knife in her hand.

"Hey, Barry!" she cried, waving the knife.

"Dry your hands on my apron, Barry," said the cook. "I been and dripped all over 'em. Come along, Barry. Take a look at my girl, Patricia, will you? I'm a proud woman. Look what I've been and done with that niece of mine. You remember the skinny sixteen-year-old bit of nothing that she was when you went away? And now will you look at her? Just like Texas beef, after it's been fattened up all summer on our good grass. She's pretty, Barry, ain't she? Her eyes get bluer and bluer every year. The boys are dyin' for her, Barry, is what they are. And won't she be making the grand wife for somebody? She's a good girl and a handy girl, Barry; but she ain't quite settled down yet. She don't know whether she's a boy or a girl, or whether her place is in the kitchen or in the saddle. But my old man used to say many a time that a hoss that didn't need some breaking wasn't no hoss at all!''

CHAPTER 3
Pantry Confidences

PATRICIA HAD SHAKEN HANDS FIRMLY WITH THE RE-
turned man and given him her best smile, but her
eyes waited and dwelt in his face.

"Come here in the pantry and talk to me while
I cut the bread and do something," she said. "Aunt
Gertie, he wants some news, and that's why he's
come in the kitchen way. Let me have him, and I'll
fill him full."

"How should he be wanting news, when you've
wrote him every week for three years, Patty?"
asked Mrs. Loomis.

"Written news," said the girl, "is no good, because you can't make any faces in a letter. Come
along, Barry."

He went into the big pantry and hoisted himself
to the top of the cracker bin. There he sat with
legs dangling, watching her swift hands at work.
She looked at him rarely, giving him only her attention and her voice, and he was able to examine
her with a tender curiosity and to nod with ap-
proval.

"I won't ask if you're glad to be back," said the girl. "I know how you feel—hard outside and hollow inside. Is that it?"

"Oh, no," he said. "I got over all the funny business in prison."

"You got all over it? You got all over what?"

"Foolish feelings," he said.

"Ah?" she said.

She lifted her head and looked not at him, but straight before her at her own thoughts.

"You were a good girl to write me once a week," he said.

"And a whole year before the first answer came," she said. She smiled a little, ruefully.

"I told you why. Solitary," said he.

"Solitary? Yes, but you never told me why they kept you in solitary confinement for a whole year. Isn't that a frightful lot?"

"It's a lot," he admitted. "They have a whole lot of hell there, besides. Rivers of it. You can get all you want there."

"Did you want it?" she asked.

"I confess that I was a little restless," he said.

"Oh, was that it? Prying around? Did that get you into trouble?"

"Punching a few fellows on the chin started the trouble. Then I got the name of being a bad actor, and I was proud of that name."

"Ah, hum," said Patricia Loomis. She added: "Go on, Barry, talk, will you? You never told me about this. What happened? How did you get out of solitary?"

"They changed wardens, and the second warden didn't believe in solitary as a punishment."

"What did he believe in?"

"Double hours of work, heavier irons, a heavier sledgehammer and plenty of beatings."

"Beatings?" said the girl, in a very quiet voice.

"Yes. They toughened me up quite a bit," he said. "I had a year of double work and short rations and plenty beatings. It makes you thin, but it keeps you in wonderful shape. You sleep without any dreams, good or bad, when you're living that sort of a life."

"Ah, hum!" said she. "But I thought that you got out on good behavior, Barry."

"Well," he said, "they'd lengthened my term four times for me under the first two wardens. They had it up to about ten years. You never heard of the trials, because I didn't write about 'em. Then the second warden was changed, when the new party was elected; and a little over a year ago, the third warden came along. He was a different cut. He wasn't holding down an easy job. He was trying to do some good. He took the bad characters out of chains. He said they simply had excess energy, and they could use it to entertain the boys every evening with boxing bouts in the prison yard. He split us up into our weights. I was a middleweight, Patty, but I got the heavyweight championship finally. I took some whalings on the way up, but I got there."

He laughed.

"Good old Barry!" said the girl.

But she frowned as she continued to cut the bread.

"Go on," she commanded.

"Well, when I won the championship—that was six months ago—the warden made me his personal trusty, his bodyguard, d'you see? There was a terrible howl from the old trusties and all the old prison officials. They said it was rewarding crime and bad behavior. But the warden stuck to me."

"Ah, there was one white man, eh?" murmured the girl.

"White man?" murmured Barry. "He was more than a white man; he was good luck to me. Then, one day, a crazy Swede tried to smash the warden's head with a crowbar; that was in the blacksmith shop. But he happened to hit my head instead. So I went to bed and, when I got out of bed, the warden was at work getting all the sentences reversed except the first one. He couldn't manage that. But he got me out inside the smallest limit of my sentence."

"God bless him!" said the girl. "But tell me this, Barry, isn't it true, when you were hit, that it wasn't by accident? You just chucked yourself into the crowbar's way, wasn't that the fact of the matter?"

"My job was to take care of the chief," said Barry, frowning a little, for the first time. "Now tell me about things around here in town. And tell me first what started you writing letters to me, Patty? We'd never known each other very well when I was here."

"It was like this," said the girl. "Everybody always had a good word for you till you went away. After that they began to shake their heads and say they always had—well, anyway, I thought that I'd write to you. And I did."

"You did," said he, soberly. "You saved my life, Patty."

"No, I didn't do that much for you," she insisted.

"I would have gone crazy that second year," said Barry Home. "I was crazy, part of the time. But your letters kept coming every week. When I got out of solitary, imagine what a heap was waiting for me—fifty letters from you to read through! I used to read 'em over and over. I could see that you were growing into a sweet youngster and getting finer all the time. About the end of the second year, they took all your letters away from me. They did that!"

His voice had not changed greatly, there was simply a new, faint ring in it. But it made Patty Loomis turn sharply upon him and catch his wrists with her strong, brown hands. He was still smiling about the mouth, but his eyes were sober and very bright.

"Don't, Barry," said the girl. "Don't act that way!"

"I'm not acting any way," said he. "I said they took your letters away from me; that was all. There were almost a hundred of 'em. I knew 'em by heart, but I used to keep on reading 'em. Nobody else wrote me any letters. Not a soul. But I could tell your letters one from another by the outside of the envelopes. Then they took 'em all away!"

Barry laughed a little. "That was not so good," he said.

She kept her hold on his wrists.

"Good old Barry," she said. "I'll tell you one thing."

"What?"

"You've got to watch yourself."

"Have I?"

"Yes."

"How should I watch myself, Patty?"

"You know what I mean. You just keep a tight hold on yourself, will you?"

"You think I might do something violent. Is that the idea?" he asked.

"That's the idea," she admitted.

"Ah, but you're wrong, Patty," said he. "I'll never do anything violent that I can be checked up for. I'll never do anything more violent than to defend myself from danger. Oh, no, I've become the most careful man in the world. Believe that?"

She kept her straight, steady glance upon him. Then she shook her head.

"Oh, Barry," she said, "they've hurt you right to the heart, haven't they?"

"Not that deep," he said. "They've just toughened my skin a little. I have a good, tough skin, now, believe me."

"I believe it," she murmured.

"Now, tell me what the picture's like here at home," he said.

"It's just the same," she answered. "I'd like to ask you a question that I never dared to put into my letters."

"You want to ask me if I robbed the stage?"

"Yes. I want to ask you that."

"I won't answer," he said.

"It wouldn't harm you to answer," she said.

He laughed cheerfully, again. "You see," he said, "I said under oath, at the trial, and I said it a good many times, that I was innocent, that I didn't rob the stage, that I didn't know where the loot was. But they chucked me into prison for three years. Two years of hell and one year of hoping. That was all. Now I talk no more about the robbing of the stage. And people won't wonder if I have money, even when I'm doing no work. There was over sixty thousand dollars in that job. I'm supposed to have it cached away, somewhere."

"Barry, what d'you mean?"

"I mean that I'm not going to work for a while. I've worked for three years hard, and now the world can work for me a while."

"There's only one way to get money without working," she said.

"No," he answered, "there are a whole lot of ways, and they're all honest, unless you're found out in the middle of the job."

She turned away from him, not answering.

"That's the way of it," he said, grimly. "Does it make you despise me, Pat?"

"No," she said, her voice trembling. "I don't despise you, but I feel pretty sick. You go and talk to Aunt Gertie for a while. I'm going to cry, or something, and be a fool."

CHAPTER 4
The First Run-in

Barry LEFT THE PANTRY AND WENT DOWN THE SHORT hall toward the dining room and lobby just as the farther door opened and young Lew Tucker strode in, facing him. It was a narrow hall with a low ceiling. Young Lew bowed his head a trifle to keep the lofty crown of his sombrero from touching the ceiling.

When he saw Home, he stopped short and stared.

Barry Home walked straight on, pausing just in front of Lew and looking up to him with that faint smile about the lips and that gravity of the eyes which was now his habitual expression.

"Hello, Lew," he said.

"Why, Barry Home!" exclaimed Lew.

"That's me," nodded Home.

"Home," said Lew Tucker, "I gotta ask you something."

"Here I am for the asking," said Home.

"I don't mean no damn joking."

"No, you don't mean any damn joking, I suppose," said Home.

Calmly he looked the big fellow up and down. A red flag in front of a bull could not have been more infuriating than this attitude of detached indifference.

Lew Tucker raised his right hand. All of it was a fist except the forefinger, which protruded, and which he now shook at the smaller man.

"Because," said Lew Tucker, "trouble is something that you might start around here, and that other folks would do the finishing of."

"Other folks are always apt to finish the trouble," nodded Barry Home, his smile unaltered.

"Are you tryin' to make a fool out of me?" asked Lew Tucker, his voice rising and turning as harsh as a rasp on metal.

"Oh, I couldn't do that," declared Barry Home. "Easy, there, Lew. It looks as though you're trying to back me out of the hall. You mustn't do that. There's room for me to squeeze by even a great big man like you!"

"I've got a mind—" said Lew.

And he turned his right hand into a complete fist by curling back the forefinger.

"You have a mind to what, Lew?" asked Barry Home, in the same amused manner.

"I gotta mind to sock you on the chin," said Lew Tucker. "I would, if you was my size. You're tryin' to make a fool out of me!"

"Now, Lew," said Barry Home, "you're a good fellow and a big fellow, but don't you think that you're making a mistake?"

"What kind of a mistake?"

"Taking a bite when you don't know whether you can swallow it or not?"

"Oh, I dunno what you mean, except you mean that you need a licking," said Lew Tucker, "and

I've a mind to give it to you. You damn, sneakin', mockin' jailbird.''

"That's all right," said Barry Home, shrugging his shoulders. "You can't irritate me, Lew. I've had men talk to me, real men with vocabularies!"

It was the final insult for Lew Tucker. Besides, he was on edge for just such a scene as this. He knew that his father was frightfully worried. He knew that the cause of the worry was this ex-convict, and he felt that any gesture he could make against Home would be against the common enemy of all his family.

So he made a half-step forward with his left foot, feinting with his left hand at the same instant, and then leaning his ponderous weight forward so that all of it came behind the whip of his right shoulder as he drove a long, straight right for the mouth of Barry Home.

These were the tactics that had won for Lew Tucker many a stiffly contested schoolyard fight. Over and over again, that feint had fooled the other fellow, and the heavy right had gone to the point. The mouth was the best target, he felt. For one thing, the lips were easily cut, and the taste of one's own blood and the sting in the numbness of the lips are disheartening. In addition, the punch is likely to stun the other fellow, so that a second and far heavier blow can often be landed with ease.

But it was not for nothing that Barry Home had fought his way up among the tough fellows of the prison yard; not for nothing had he fought thrice with "Tiger" Humphries, the ex–prize–fighter, for the heavyweight championship of the jail! Twice they had fought out twenty desperate rounds to a draw. The third time, he knew the Tiger's tricks by heart, and a merciful referee stopped the slaughter in the fifth round.

A fellow like Lew Tucker, big as he was, was

merely a much easier target. Barry Home let the feint go. The serious purpose, he knew, was in the following right. When that punch came, he flattened himself against the wall and let it shoot past his face.

Lew Tucker bumped into a short right jab which was as solid as the projecting fork of a tree. It hurt his ribs and took his breath. He twitched to the side and, clubbing his big left fist, smashed it downward at the restless head of Barry Home. The smaller man stepped inside that punch and heaved all his weight into a flying uppercut that landed just under the chin of the big fellow.

Lew Tucker did not pitch back. His head jerked convulsively with the impact; then he fell on his face as though a trip hammer had fallen on the back of his brain. He lay still, with his arms stretched out before him and the fingers twitching. Otherwise, there was no movement.

Barry opened the door into the lobby. Straight before him he saw the sheriff, Bert Wayland, in earnest conversation with Rance Tucker.

"Hello, Tucker! Hello, Sheriff Wayland!" said he. "Won't you come and take a look at poor Lew, here? He's had an accident. He must have slipped and fallen on his chin. He's knocked out!"

Rance Tucker went back a full stride, as he heard that voice, his eyes opened and let Barry Home look deep into his soul, to see all that he had suspected that he might find there—stark, staring guilt.

However, Tucker ran forward into the hall, and Barry Home heard him exclaiming over the fallen body of his son. Then Lew Tucker began to groan and make feeble, kicking motions with his legs.

The other men in the lobby hurried forward to enjoy the scene, waving and nodding greeting askance to Barry Home as they went by him.

Only the sheriff remained where he had been before, and he said tersely: "Kind of like an entrance in a play, ain't it, Barry?"

"The villain's entrance, d'you mean?" said Barry Home.

The sheriff glanced quickly at him. "How d'you mean that?" he asked.

"Why, I always mean what's right. I never mean any offense," said the other.

Wayland thrust out his jaw.

"I wanta talk to you, my friend," said he. "And I guess there's no better time for talking than right now."

"I can't think of a better time," said Barry Home, "except over a glass of whisky. Step into the bar and have one with me?"

Wayland thrust out his chin still farther.

"You've got yourself all polished up smooth and smart while you been away these three years, ain't you?" he asked.

"I've had a good deal of grooming and dressing down. I ought to be polished enough to shine, sheriff," he said.

He smiled, as though expecting sympathetic comment from the other, but Wayland was only angrier than before.

"You wanta watch yourself and your step, now that you're back here," he said.

"In a rough country, a man always has to watch the ground under him," agreed Barry Home, gently.

"What I mean," said the sheriff, "you wanta look out for yourself. Right now you been slugging Lew Tucker, have you? You're gonna try and ride the Tuckers, are you, because old man Rance told the truth about you and landed you in stripes?"

"My dear sheriff," said the other, "I never pick a fight. I really never do. I've had enough fighting to last me the rest of my life. But I don't mind taking on the trouble that's brought to me by others. I dare say you know what I mean."

"You 'dare say' that I do, eh?" said the sheriff, snarling and growing angrier as he listened. "You been and worked up your language a lot while you was away, did you?"

"I read a few books, if you don't mind," said Barry Home. "They had an excellent library at the prison. It wasn't a bad place at all, as a matter of fact."

Sheriff Wayland grunted.

"Perhaps you'll see it, someday," suggested Barry Home.

"Meaning that I'll be sent up, eh?" exclaimed Wayland. "Now, look a'here, young feller, if you think that you can start badgering me, I'll tell you this: I'm here to keep Loomis peaceful tonight. And peaceful is what it's gunna be. You hear me talk?"

"I hear you talk," agreed the other.

"Well, you keep right on hearing, then!"

"Thank you," said Barry Home, "I'll keep right on hearing, sheriff."

"Mocking me, are you?" shouted the sheriff, suddenly.

"Why, who am I to mock the sheriff of the county?" asked Barry Home, opening his eyes as though in smiling and polite surprise.

"I see your line," said the sheriff, crimson with anger. "And maybe—hey, Lew Tucker!"

Lew Tucker was on his feet, at last, looking stunned and settling his hat on his head with one hand, while with the other he fumbled at a small bleeding place on his chin.

"Well?" muttered young Tucker.

"Did this gent jump you, Lew?" asked the sheriff. "Go on and tell us what happened. Breaking the peace is enough to slam folks in jail in this here neck of the woods!"

But Lew Tucker, making no answer, his eyes darkly fixed before him, simply strode across the lobby. A minute later his footfall sounded heavily on the veranda outside and he was gone.

CHAPTER 5
Drink It Down!

Rance followed his son to the door, which he jerked open, and leaning out, bawled loudly: "Hey, Lew, Lew! Come back in here, will you?"

There was no answer from Lew Tucker, but from the night came the whistle of the storm, hooting like an owl in the distance and then whistling high and small, near at hand. A gust of icy wind entered and caught a paper from the floor, sending it hurrying in tatters until it flattened against the glowing body of the big stove. There the paper began to smoke, and Dave Loomis caught it up and folded it against his fat stomach, saying:

"Now, Rance, just close that door, will you? It looks like Lew had had a kind of a fall, and he ain't likely to come back inside here and face all the folks for a while. I'm sorry about that, too, because Lew is a good scout. But you know how it is, when you're kind of proud. A young gent, he don't like to stumble over nothing and get a fall, not even over a Barry Home!"

Rance Tucker closed the door and turned about.

His face was pale; even in that instant the strength of the rising wind had blown a film across his eyes. Now, looking down, he brushed from his knees a few glistening flakes of snow. They turned to water at the touch of his hand. He flicked the drops away and shook his head, with the air of one who is striving vainly to solve a problem of immense depth and importance.

When he looked up, at last, his glance fell upon Barry Home and hastily jerked away from him, again.

The sheriff lifted his voice.

"What I wanta know," he said, "is did Barry Home jump Lew Tucker, out there in the hall. If he did, I'm gunna do something about it!"

No one answered.

Wayland, with a shrug of his shoulders, growled out: "You've gone and turned yourself into a fox, have you, Barry Home? But foxes can't last long in a place like Loomis!"

"Of course not!" agreed Barry Home.

He made the gesture of one deprecating all hard feeling and withdrawing all opposition.

"I told you what happened," he said. "Poor Lew just stumbled and fell on his chin. That's hard luck and I'm sorry."

Dave Loomis went up to him and laid a fat, brown, red-backed hand upon his shoulder.

"You go and be a good scout, will you, Barry?"

"Why, of course, I'll be a good scout," said Barry Home. "I've learned how you're punished when you're bad in this world, and now I'm going to be good. I'm going to work night and day to be good, of course. You would, too, if you'd had three years of the strict teaching that I've been through."

The whole crowd was listening to these words, as it gathered more and more closely to the stove.

This was the first of the really cold weather. In the morning, they might awake in a white world, one that would stay white for five long months. Later on, they would grow acclimated to the cold, but now the drafts worked up sleeves and trouser legs, and down inside neckbands like little fingers of ice. It was a moment when women could stop regretting that their work was over a hot stove; it was a moment when the hotel keeper seemed the luckiest man in the world. Some of those men would be out riding range in the dusk of the next morning, their horses slipping through slush or sliding on well-iced surfaces. They were downhearted, now, thinking about what lay before them, wondering why they had chosen this country to live in and how the summer could fly away so fast.

So they gathered near the stove, edging toward it, turning their shoulders to the heat, stretching out furtive hands to it, as though it were a solid thing of value that could be stolen and kept in one's possession.

In the meantime, they listened to Barry Home's pleasant and unexcited voice, as he spoke to Dave Loomis and pronounced the values of a life in prison.

"Now, Barry," said Dave, "don't you go and laugh behind my back!"

"He ain't laughin' behind your back; he's laughin' in your face," said the sheriff. "I dunno what I oughta do about him. I dunno but what I oughta lock him up, right now, and by the jumpin' Jiminy, I think that I'm gonna do it!"

"Why, I wouldn't do that," said the voice of one who had just stepped into the lobby from the barroom.

That was the tall, elegant form of Tom London, his silken scarf adjusted neatly now, his clothes

33

well brushed, his boots polished, his whole manner alert, genial, gentlemanly. He was smoking a cigarette, and the very way in which he flicked off the ash pronounced him to be a man of taste and of understanding.

The sheriff turned sharply on this man of strange and suspicious character.

"Are you turnin' yourself into a judge, Tom?" he asked.

But his words were spoken in a complaining rather than an insulting tone.

"I'm not a judge," said Tom London. "But I remember that they always used to say in this part of the country, in the old days, that one never should kick a dog when he's down."

"That's good. That's right," said Dave Loomis. "Now, mix around, everybody. Step into the bar and everybody's gonna have a drink on the house, in honor of Barry Home getting back to us. Come on, Barry, and we'll lead the way!"

With that, he took the arm of Barry Home, and so violently interrupted the argument and the wrath of the sheriff. The latter followed thoughtfully toward the end of the line. He found Tom London beside him, and muttered: "What would you be takin' his part for, Tom? You think that it ain't too late to make a friend out of him?"

"Oh, I'm not thinking about that," answered Tom London. "I don't so much care whether he's friendly or not. He's not apt to be so friendly, because he tried to put the blame for the Crystal Creek robbery on my shoulders. You know how it is, sheriff. Men always hate the people that they've wronged. So I suppose that he hates me. But that's all right. I can take care of myself, I hope, even when there's a Barry Home about."

The sheriff looked curiously at his companion.

He, in common with the rest of the community, had his doubts about London's source of income. Nevertheless, he was interested in the truth of the last remarks.

"He's changed," said he.

"Of course, he's changed," said London. "Prison changes men."

"Yeah, it changes every one of 'em."

"It doesn't often improve them, to be sure," said London.

"No, it don't," admitted the sheriff. "That's the bad part of it. You'd say that prison is a thing that had oughta improve a gent. If it takes him when he's bad and makes him worse, then what good is it?"

"Prison," said Tom London, "is like hammering in a blacksmith shop. You put the hot iron on the anvil, and then you beat it. Sometimes you beat too hard, and you crystallize it. Then it's brittle, and won't hold any edge. It breaks when it's most needed. But sometimes the hammering works up a perfect temper. I'd say that Barry has more of a cutting edge, right now."

"Every Home has had a cutting edge," muttered the sheriff. "I'm worried, is what I am. I'm worried mighty bad. I don't like the way that he looks. I don't even like the way that he smiles!"

"Oh, that's all right," said Tom London. "He's feeling a little strange, just now. Everybody feels strange and upset when they come out of jail. That's only natural."

"Here we are having a drink to him. That's kind of funny," said the sheriff. "I dunno that I oughta drink to him, though."

"Do what the rest do," said Tom London. "That's the easy way out of everything."

He smiled as he said it, but the sheriff sighed. Sheriff Wayland was the most honest man in the world, and one of the bravest, but he was not exceedingly clever, and now, as he had admitted, he was very worried, indeed.

They filed into the barroom with the others. The bar was thickly lined.

Then, Dave Loomis said: "Fill 'em up, boys. There's the glasses, and there's the whisky bottles. Help yourselves and fill 'em high. Speakin' personal, it's a good day for me when Barry Home comes back. His father and his grandfather before him, I knew 'em both, and they knew me. Barry's had his bad luck. We all know about that, and there ain't any doubt that the best thing is to forget about it and take Barry for what he was before ever anybody doubted him. Barry, I'm lookin' at you."

"Wait a minute," said Barry Home.

He held up his hand. Every glass was frozen in place, most of them halfway to the lips, as Barry spoke:

"I want to say this, fellows. Dave Loomis is a kind man, and always was a kind man. I'm glad to drink his liquor and to drink to him. But I've got to say that I suspect a good many of the people in the room are not exactly friendly to me. That's all right. I don't expect them to be. But I'd simply like to know where I stand. If there's a single fellow here who doesn't feel that he's my friend or that I can be his friend, I wish that he wouldn't take this drink."

He looked carefully about the room and a battery of eyes was turned upon the faces of Rance Tucker and Tom London.

Rance Tucker seemed to be in a quandary. He raised the glass, and he lowered it. He stared straight ahead of him, then flicked his glance to either side, like a speaker stuck for want of the right word.

In the meantime, however, Tom London said, cheerfully: "It's all right, Barry. I suppose that you have some bad thoughts about me, but I have none about you. Here's to you! Here's in your eye, Barry Home!''

With a fine, flourishing gesture, he downed the glass of drink. Rance Tucker, with a sigh of relief, followed his example.

CHAPTER 6
Frank Talk

THE DELIGHT OF DAVE LOOMIS OVERFLOWED. HE beamed upon the entire company, his face reddening as he looked about him. While he cheered on the festivities, other men ordered drinks, the constraint disappeared from the faces of nearly all, and even the sheriff seemed to be relaxing.

As for Tom London, he walked up to Barry Home and the latter met him in a corner of the room, smiling. Tom held out his hand. Barry took it instantly.

"I'm glad that you've done that, Barry," said the man of mystery. "After what your ideas were at the trial, I thought that there might be some black blood in your heart."

"Because you shifted the blame for the robbery on my shoulders?" said Home, calmly.

"Come, come, Barry," said the other. "You don't stick to that point of view, do you?"

"Come, come, Tom," said Barry. "Where's your sense of humor? When you say that, can't you smile a little?"

They spoke quietly. People three yards away could not make out what was being said. The more vital the words, the lower the pitch in which they were spoken.

"You never explained your theory to me," said Tom London, his eyes frank and curious. "What is it?"

"Are you still riding the same horse?" asked Home. "The big dappled chestnut, I mean."

"The very same," said Tom London.

"The same one whose trail led from the place of the robbery of the Crystal Creek coach?"

"You mean," said London, smiling tolerantly, "that the horse's trail was like the chestnut's? There was the same barred shoe on the near front hoof. The chestnut had a touch of frog, you know. Never bothers him now, but I keep the barred shoe on him, just in case."

"My theory is this," said the young man. "You and Tucker probably had your horses shod in the same shop here. Why not? Tucker's gray mustang with the barred shoe on the near front hoof and yours. That was odd enough to cause the two of you to comment on it. Now, then, when you heard that they were on the trail of your horse, after the robbery, you remembered the gray mustang that also had the barred front hoof. Isn't that simple?"

"So far it sounds simple enough, if it were true," said Tom London. "Go on, old son, I like to see the way your brain works."

"All right," said Barry Home. "I don't mind showing you just how my head works, Tom. My idea is this: As soon as you heard they were on your trail, you got hold of Tucker, and made a proposition to him. If he would run the blame for the robbery onto somebody else, then you would give him a good split of the profits of the robbery. Maybe ten or fifteen thousand!"

"Ah? Go on, Barry. You work it out so smoothly

that I almost begin to believe that I must have done something like that," said Tom London.

"Of course, you did," said the ex-convict. "And then you easily worked out the details of the rest of the story with him. Nothing hard about that, I should say! In the first place, he got up in the middle of the night or early in the morning, to fit in better. He happened to hear a horse snort and he looked out the window and saw the gray mustang being ridden into the corral. The corral gate squeaked. He waited there at the window, and saw the rider clearly. It was Barry Home, the same Barry Home whom Rance Tucker had begun to hate because he lost so much money to me at seven-up, whenever he had a game in the evening. That's the story, Tom, and after the story was cooked up, you got Rance Tucker to stick to it."

"It's a good enough story," said Tom London. "I remember that your lawyer tried to work up your case along those lines, though, so I'm not surprised to hear it now."

"No, you're not very surprised," he answered. "I simply wanted you to know that I stand on the same ground, but more strongly."

"What's given more strength to your case?" asked Tom London.

"Why," said Barry Home, "haven't you looked into the eyes of poor Rance Tucker tonight?"

"What about 'em?" said London.

"They're as blank as the eyes of an owl at midday, but there's a little red glitter rising up in 'em from time to time."

"What does that tell you, Barry?"

"Why, that he's half crazy. That's what it tells me, Tom. What does it tell you?"

"Simply that he knows that a Barry Home is a dangerous man to have for an enemy, and that he's going to watch you, to keep from being hurt. But you don't mean to say that you really still stick to the theory of the frame between me and Rance Tucker, do you?"

"Yes, I still stick to that."

"By thunder!" muttered Tom London, suddenly.

"Well?"

"I wonder if I have it!"

"Have what?"

"Why, the right theory and I think I have, Barry. It's humped right into the middle of my brain, and I'll swear that it's right."

"Fire away."

"I'd better wait and try to work this up."

"Just as you please."

"Well, I might as well tell you what I'm guessing," said Tom London. "It's this, that Rance Tucker himself may have drifted over and stuck up that stage!"

"Ah?" said the young fellow.

"That's what I mean. Think it over. It fits together well enough. Rance Tucker may have wanted a bit of extra hard cash. I never knew a rancher in my life who didn't need hard cash."

"He had some payments coming due, about that time, but they were only for four or five thousand dollars," said the young fellow.

"That's all right. He couldn't have known that that particular stage was so loaded down with gold, could he?"

"Go on," said Barry Home.

"Why, that's all there is to it. He's in a little pinch. He decides that he'll work himself out of it with a gun instead of with mortgages and banks. So he takes the gray and rides over and turns the trick."

"I could understand that," agreed Barry Home, nodding his head.

"Of course, you could understand it. And Rance Tucker was a rough devil when he was a youngster. There are plenty of stories floating around about his work in the old days. Oh, in a pinch he can be a fighting man."

Barry Home nodded, but with a frown that carried no conviction whatsoever.

"Then," argued Tom London, "listen to the rest."

"I'm listening, all right."

"Why, the day after the robbery, he hears that they're on the trail of his horse with the barred shoe and that drives him crazy with fear. He decides that he'll hang the blame on you, because he doesn't like you. That's all there is to it!"

Barry Home looked into a shadowy corner of the ceiling, like a man conceiving a distant and difficult thought.

Then he shook his head again.

"Rance Tucker," he said, "is more the type of fellow who fights when his back is against the wall, or when he's half crazy—when he's drunk, say, or when he's pinched in a tight corner and can't get out. Then he could be a devil, I suppose. I saw him cornered by his big red bull in a field one day, and he laid the bull out by pulling up a loose fence post and slamming the bull over the head with it. He could fight, but he wouldn't go out to do a trick like the stage robbery."

"He was in a corner," said London. "He needed the money. That's enough of a corner to make him rob a stage, I guess."

"Maybe, maybe," murmured Barry Home. "I'm glad that you suggested it, at any rate, because I want to go over everything fairly."

Tom London suddenly narrowed his eyes. "You've got something on your mind, Barry, of course," he said.

"Yes, I've got something to do," said the other.

"Well, good luck to you."

"I'm going to tell you what it is, too," said Barry

Home. "You've talked frankly to me, and I'm going to talk frankly to you."

"That's the straight thing to do," said Tom London. "Particularly if you've got something against me."

"Why, it's this way," said Barry Home. "I spent three years in the pen."

"Of course, I know that."

"And I went up for a job that I didn't do."

Tom London nodded. His interest was intense, so that his jaw set hard and his nostrils flared a little.

"Three years is a long time," went on the boy. "It's such a long time, that I decided, while I was in the prison, that I'd get the man or the men who had railroaded me."

"That's natural," commented the other. "I suppose every fellow in the same situation feels the same."

"And swore by everything holy that I'd never give up the trail."

"That's swearing by a lot."

"It is. And it means a lot," he replied. "And that's why I'm telling you, London. In spite of what you've said, I still think you may have had a hand in the job. When I find out the truth, if you're in it, I'm going to do my best to send you west."

"That's frank," nodded London.

"It is," agreed the young man. "It makes a square deal and a fair fight between us. If you can cover up your trail, good. That is, if your trail needs covering. Otherwise, I'll run down the devil who railroaded me and I'll kill him. What happens to me after that, I don't care."

Tom closed his eyes as he nodded.

"You mean business," he said, soberly. "And I don't blame you. I'm thanking you for telling me that I'm still on the suspected list."

He held out his hand, and for the second time that evening Barry Home gripped it firmly.

CHAPTER 7
A Gesture

LONDON DRIFTED TO ANOTHER PART OF THE BARROOM. And Barry Home now had the attention of Dave Loomis himself. A big man was Dave and fairly well blocked the eyes of Barry from the rest of the room, yet, with side glances, he managed to keep track of most of the movements of the others in the place.

Prison experience helped him here, the sort of experience that enables a criminal, at one of the long dining tables, to catch the attention of another criminal with a single glance, and then to carry on a complicated conversation by means of signals made with the head, gesture of the hand, and a few significant words tapped out in a code with a spoon against a plate or a cup, all done in the most haphazard way imaginable. With the farthest corners of the senses, as it were, Barry Home had learned to note matters in detail, though with the most inconsiderable glance of the eyes.

It seemed to Dave Loomis that Home was giving him his full attention; but as a matter of fact, he was studying all the crowd, either from side to side, or with glimpses over the shoulder of Loomis into the long mirror that extended down the bar.

It was in that reflection that he saw Tom London pass Rance Tucker, far down the room, and let his arm graze against the side of the rancher.

Rance Tucker paid no heed, apparently.

But surface indications are another thing that convicts learn to disregard. When, a moment later, Tucker finished his drink and left the room, Barry did not hesitate.

He walked out into the lobby in time to see the broad back of Rance Tucker disappearing through a door that led onto the side veranda. He could not directly follow without calling too much attention to himself, because every man in the room was sure to be aware of the bad blood that existed between himself and Tucker.

But why had Tucker gone out there into the whirling snow of the storm?

The cold was growing momently more bitter. The draft that flowed under the doors and across the floor was like a stream of ice water. People were continually shifting their position and shrugging the shoulders of their coats into different wrinkles. Why should Rance Tucker step out of the hotel to the southern veranda?

Well, there would be shelter, here, from the full blast of the wind, for one thing, more than on any other side of the house. In addition to that, it was the side nearest to the stable. If a man were suddenly to decide to go out and hitch up his horses, he might go either through the back hall and around the corner, or straight over the southern veranda.

Barry passed through the hall that led in such a narrow compass past the dining room. He would have avoided the pantry, but, as he was stepping by it, the door flew open and the girl, with a loaded tray, stepped out before him.

When she saw him, she came to a halt, with her head held stiff and high, and her eyes darkening soberly at him.

"Barry," she said, "are you getting ready to raise the devil around here?"

"I'll never raise the devil again," said he. "I'll never be breaking the law, Patty."

He would have taken the weight of the tray from her. She shook her head and frowned to warn him to get back.

"I don't trust you, Barry," she said. "You've started on poor Lew Tucker, already."

"Why," he said, "you know how that happened, don't you?"

"Yes, I know," she answered, gloomily. "He tripped and fell down on his chin. Wasn't that just it?"

"You could believe it, if you wanted to," he said.

"Show me the backs of your hands," she commanded.

He held them out, obediently.

"How did you get that welt across your fingers, just in front of the knuckles, Barry?" she asked.

"As I was walking down the road," he said, promptly, "I was swinging my hands to make the walking easier and keep up my circulation. You know, the wind was cold."

"I know the wind was cold," she said, eying him carefully.

"As I was swinging my hands, this one whacked across a stripped branch that was sticking out of some shrubbery."

"Where did it happen?"

"Down at the beginning of the trees."

"The shrubbery's on the left down there, coming this way," said the girl.

"Perhaps it happened further up toward the hotel," he said.

"Perhaps," she answered. Then she added: "Look here, Barry, whatever else it was, it wasn't good sense to tackle Lew Tucker. It let everybody know that you're on the warpath. If anything happens, you're going to be jailed for it. Anything!"

"I know that, and that's why nothing is going to happen," he said.

"Oh, Barry," murmured the girl, "you're going to smash things up, I know. You're going to ruin your own life, for one thing!"

He slid a hand under the tray and took the weight of it.

"I'm not going to break the law," he insisted.

"But what are you going to do?"

"Make an easy living."

"Easy livings are not honest. That's the fact of the matter."

"Look at the way your Uncle Dave lives here," said he. "That's both easy and honest, I'd say."

She shook her head at him, frowning with pain.

"You don't mean that sort of living," said she. "I know that you don't!"

"I've made up my mind," he answered. "You see how it turns out."

"I feel pretty sick about you, Barry," she replied.

At this, the faint smile disappeared utterly from his face.

"Pat," he said, "do you give a rap?"

"I give several raps," she said and nodded.

"Really?"

"Yes."

"You mean that you—that you—well, that you really care about me, Pat?"

"Why should I say so?"

"You shouldn't. I know that you shouldn't."

Then he added: "I told you that there was a time

when your letters were the only thing that kept me from going crazy. I meant that. I mean it now when I say that if I could put the world in a balance, with you on the other side, you'd outweigh the rest of the world for me, Pat."

"You were always a good, friendly sort of a liar, Barry," she answered.

"Don't you think that I mean it?"

"Not a whack," she said.

"I tell you, it's true."

"Prove it," she said.

"There's a tray between us," said he. "Otherwise—"

"I don't mean foolishness. I mean, you really step out and prove it, Barry; will you?

"What sort of a reward is there at the end of the trail?" he asked her.

"There's that better half of the world that you were talking about a while ago."

He straightened to his full height, his shoulders hunched a little forward, in the attitude of one prepared to receive the shock of a very heavy blow.

"You're talking about yourself, Pat?"

"I'm doing that. Are you interested?"

"Give me a chance to prove it, Pat. That's all I ask for. Except that I'm a dog if I let you care about me now."

"I wrote to you for three years because I thought you were getting a bad deal," she told him. "I thought you were the underdog and that your life was ruined. Then you came back here to-night and I could tell after one look that your life wasn't ruined. No, no, you are a lot more apt to dig in and do some ruining on your own account!

"I liked you before, and now the trouble that I feel on account of you, Barry, is aching away inside me every moment. If you honestly wanted me, you could have me in a minute, Barry. I'd go around the world blacking your boots. I'm not proud. But if you want me, you've simply got to go straight."

"What do you mean by going straight?" he asked her.

"Being an honest man in the eyes of God and yourself. What do you mean by going straight?"

"Never bringing myself to the attention of the law. That's what going straight means, to the rest of the world."

She shook her head.

"I knew that it was something like that. You've been hurt and now you're going to pass the kick along. Give me the tray at once, Barry."

"Are you going to walk out on me like this?" he asked her.

"I'm not walking out on you. It's only that I saw the poison in you; that's all. If you're not honest, Barry, I wouldn't follow you around the world. I wouldn't follow you one step. Not if you were the King of England!"

"Sunday school stuff rubs out and wears thin, before the finish," he said.

"This idea of mine won't rub out and wear thin," she assured him. "It's as close to my heart as my blood is."

"You're thinking of children and all that, eh?" he asked her.

"That's what I'm mostly thinking about," said the girl. "Let me go by, Barry."

"Wait one minute longer," he pleaded.

"Well?"

"I'm going to think over what you've said," he declared.

"You say that you'll think it over. But you don't mean it. You've made up your mind already. Somebody's going to die for the years you spent in jail. Rance Tucker or Tom London, perhaps. I know what you have in your mind. Everybody knows, for that matter!"

He sighed, and stepped back.

"You think you're walking out of my life, Pat," he said. "but you can't. If you care a whit about this jailbird, he's going to keep you caring."

She uttered a short exclamation and hurried past him down the hall.

CHAPTER 8
In the Barn

THERE WAS IN BARRY HOME A COLD DEVIL THAT HAD been born three years before and nourished by the brutal cruelty and injustice he had received during the intervening time. It was generally the topmost spirit in his breast, but now for an instant it shrank down and died within him, and all that was kind and warmhearted in him sprang alive.

He had almost cried out to her. If he had done so and she had turned to show him the suffering in her face, he would have been changed forever.

But he did not cry out. He saw her push open the swinging door of the dining room and again he strove to speak, but again the devil in him throttled the words and they were unspoken.

As the door swung shut behind her, making a faint moaning sound upon the rusting hinges, he sighed. With that sigh the kindlier impulses died out of his heart and left it cold and calm again.

She was gone from his sight.

Yet for a moment he laid his hand against the

side of the wall and considered. It seemed to him that he could see her more clearly than ever, not only face and body as they were, but as if through a veil of glowing flesh and blood, the whole spirit, and all that he saw of her was gentle and true, brave and womanly. Yet, the impulse which already had been mastered in him once would not master him again, so quickly. He turned down the hall once more.

His business was not with women, no matter how fine they might be. His business was what he had promised himself that it would be, one day in the frightful darkness of the solitary cell, when he was eating out his heart. No—the truth is no heart was left in him on that day, when the dark, cold panic of the grave had overcome him in a rush and he had wished to fling himself at the door, screaming for mercy, for help, and for freedom, one glimpse of the fine, pure light of the day!

Then, when he had mastered that desire to surrender, as he grimly took hold of himself with the last iron atom of willpower that was left to him, he had gone down on his knees and promised that he would do certain things, when his term expired, if that time ever came!

During the remainder of his imprisonment, every trouble was easier to bear, even when he looked forward to a prolonged term, for he felt that he had been to the bottom of the pit, and that thereafter nothing could wring the sinews of his soul as they had been wrung before. To him, the promise of what he would accomplish when freedom came was like the hope of spring in the dim, cold heart of winter.

So that unforgotten moment came back over him again and, turning down the hall, he went swiftly to the back of the hotel and out through an entrance not far from the kitchen door.

As he stepped into the open, the wind cut at him

with a saber stroke, its cold edge penetrating to the nerve and the bone.

But what of it? Very little, indeed, to a man who had been manacled in a blizzard with a twelve-pound sledgehammer to swing to keep himself warm and with a rock pile to use his energy upon.

He merely shrugged his shoulders, rested his hand for an instant against the wall, already snow-incrusted, and looked out toward the barn.

There was one dim light glowing in it, showing through the cracks around one of the windows. If he followed that light, perhaps he would find Rance Tucker. And might not Tom London be with the rancher?

He went at a run, sprinting lightly along. And so he came to the corner of the barn and paused, with the wind beating about him. There was not much snow falling, and that was so very dry that it shook off from his clothes at a shrug of his shoulders, but it added to the biting cold of the first winter blizzard.

There was a sliding door at either end of the barn, as he knew. But he could not risk pushing open the one nearest him. Little by little, he worked it back, but only the fraction of an inch. Then, staring through, he made out suddenly the face of Rance Tucker, not a yard away!

He almost cried out, in his astonishment and bewilderment, at this sudden apparition. Looking again, he saw that Rance was alone, sitting upon the grain bin, whittling long, thin slivers from a stick of wood and scowling thoughtfully at his work.

Beyond him, extended the long line of horses in their stalls, a dozen of them, at least. What was the meaning of this lonely vigil of Rance Tucker?

Barry could not enter the barn on this side to find out and, if he remained there in the open to spy on the man, he would soon be frozen.

He ran to the other side of the barn, pushed open the other sliding door a little and looked into the thick, solid velvet of utter darkness.

That was what he wanted and, slipping inside, he pushed the door shut behind him.

Then, closing his eyes, he tried to remember exactly what this side of the barn had been like in the old days. It might have changed in the interim but, as it was before, there had been horse stalls part of the way and other stalls at the farther end where cows were kept in the bitterest of the winter cold. At each end crosspieces nailed to big uprights that fenced in the mow led upward to the top of the mow.

Yes, he could remember all of that very clearly.

Ahead of him, he heard horses stamping and snorting as they worked their muzzles deeper into the feed of the mangers; wet horses, for he could detect the unmistakable odor.

Feeling down the wall to his left, he reached the side of the mow and presently located the ladder that led upward. Up that he climbed, with the hay bulging out and scratching him as he worked on. But now there was vacancy before him. He reached out, probed empty space, and found that he had come to the top of the hay.

He stepped from the ladder, and sank to his knees in the soft fluff. It was sweet to his nostrils, and the place was gratefully warm, as though some of the heat of the long summer had been harvested and kept there with the hay, to prepare for the savage length of approaching winter.

He was not conscious of a light at first but, standing quite still for a moment, he finally was able to make out a dim glow from the farther side of the mow. That would be the lantern which was burning there, giving Rance Tucker enough light for his whittling that was now being so very thoughtfully conducted.

He began to cross the top of the mow, but presently collided with something that barked his shins. He fell forward, and hard, cold iron slithered up the side of his neck.

Lying still, feeling about him, he discovered that he had tripped over a big pitchfork, left lying on its back with spear-pointed, tiger-toothed prongs sticking up two feet and a half.

One of them might have passed well enough through his throat; one of them might have glided easily through his heart; and that would have been the end of his endeavors in this world!

He sat up, after a little time, and smiled faintly in that darkness. It was a very odd world, to be sure. The dangers that are plotted with human cunning may be far smaller, indeed, than the dangers that are cast in one's path by chance.

At last, he stood up, and went forward again. His feet accustomed themselves, as of old, to the art of walking in deep hay, which consists in taking short steps, as when walking through soft sand, and waiting for the resilient rebound of the compressed hay to lift and help one forward. He smiled again, remembering how he had worked, on a time, stowing away hay in that very barn.

Patty Loomis had been a mere youngster of eleven, at that time, and hardly worth the notice of a fully matured man sixteen years old. He had been very proud to work with experienced laborers making hay. He had been praised for his ability to pitch from the ground to the wagon. He had been praised, most of all, for his willingness to work on top of the stack inside the barn, and stow it away under the roof, with no breath of air stirring and the dreadful heat of the sun pouring through the shingles of the roofing above him.

He had been praised for that. He smiled as he remembered the big Irishman who, leaning on his hayfork, had called to the others.

"Look at Barry, now, will you? He's a whale, when he gets on the end of a pitchfork, is what he is. For the size of him I never seen such a lifter!"

Oh, they had worked him hard enough, in those days of his youth. Yet it had been a pleasant time for Barry Home. How he had gloried in the excess of his strength as he never would glory again until that happy day when his hands were on the throat of the man who had engineered his trip to the prison—Rance Tucker or Tom London; one of that pair or both! He hardly cared which.

Then, stepping on, he came close to the edge of the mow. It was difficult to come to the very side of it, for the hay on top of the mow, being the loosest, was very apt to slide beneath a weight, and might throw him down into the manger below, a most excellent way of breaking bones!

So he lay down flat and, inching forward, at last was able to part a projecting tuft of the hay and stare down at the scene beneath him.

Rance Tucker had not moved, apparently. The heads of the horses were almost entirely lost in the shadows made by the stall partitions. One of the mustangs, perhaps outworn by a long day's work or else a very fast eater, was lying down already.

Then the sliding door of the barn opened, and Tom London stepped inside.

CHAPTER 9
Thieves' Conference

"T HOUGHT YOU'D CHANGED YOUR MIND ABOUT COMING out," said Rance Tucker. "Wasn't it here that you said meet you, in case there was a need of us talking?"

"I said the woodshed," said Tom London, "but when I didn't find you there, I came on out here."

"Well?" said Tucker.

"Nobody else around here?"

"Nobody," said Tucker.

Tom London lifted his head and looked straight at the spot where the boy was lying at the edge of the mow above him.

"A barn is a damned silly place to talk in," he said. "A thousand men could be hidden away within earshot of us."

"Yeah, and who would be hidden away on a night like this with the Loomis stoves going so fine and the Loomis whisky so good?" asked Rance Tucker.

"One man would," answered Tom London.

"You mean the kid?"

"He's not a kid any longer," said London.

"Aw, damn him!" said Tucker.

He shut his knife with a click. "I'm tired of thinkin' about him," he concluded.

"So am I," said London.

"Well?" asked Tucker.

The outthrust jaw made his head tilt back a little, so that Barry could examine his face more clearly.

It was not an ugly face, really, but a face that showed hard endeavor and a strong will, yet unbroken by life. He seemed to await suggestions.

"You saw me talking to him?" asked London.

"Yeah, I seen you, and you seemed to be having a good time out of it. I wonder what he did to Lew? How'd he manage to handle Lew, I wonder."

"He's strong," said London. "I tell you, he was a soft kid when he went to prison, but he's had three years of hell. You can see the whole of the three years in his eyes, if you look!"

"I looked into 'em, right enough," declared Tucker. "There wasn't no other place that a man could look. It was like facin' a double-barreled shotgun, I tell you!"

"Worse," said London. "A lot worse. And he'd kill quicker and more surely than a double-barreled shotgun, too!"

"I'll put my faith in a shotgun even agin' Barry Home," said Tucker. "I wonder what he could've done to Lew?"

"Why, hit him out of time, that's all. Lew didn't stop to argue. He just left."

"He'll be back. He's got pride, that Lew of mine has," declared the father, gloomily. "And he'll be back, mind you, London. You can bet on that!"

"I'm glad that he's coming back," said London. "But he's young, Rance."

"He's young, but he's a man."

"Nobody's a man till he's thirty," said London,

with conviction, "or until he's had a few years in prison, someplace."

"You got both them advantages, maybe?" asked Tucker, with a twisted grin.

London looked down at the other without answering and, though his face was utterly in shadow, Barry could guess that he was smiling.

"This is pretty far west to be asking so many questions," said London.

"Maybe that's true," said the rancher.

He added: "What was you talkin' to Barry Home so hard and fast about?"

"I was trying to change his mind for him."

"Change his mind about what? About you being the robber?"

Tucker actually laughed and, as he listened, the mirth ran like a freezing poison through the body of the listener.

"That wasn't his idea," said London.

"No?"

"No, it wasn't."

"Couldn't the young fool see that?" asked Tucker.

"He couldn't. He's had three years to think everything over, and that's too long for a brain of his sort, I suppose."

"He's got a good enough brain to handle Lew," scowled Tucker, unable to forget his son's unhappy experience. "What is his idea?"

"That you turned the trick, by yourself."

"Is that what he thinks?"

"Yes, that's what he thinks."

Barry Home listened with interest to the lie. He could see the point of it, clearly. A queer sense of omniscience came over him, and he began to guess that his theory about the robbery had been entirely accurate.

Rance Tucker slid from the top of the feed box

and stood shaking his fist at the air—also, in the direction of the man he was cursing!

"Damn that fool!" said he. "Why would he think that I'd do a thing like that, and me a respectable rancher and everything."

"He was working for you, then."

"A lazy, worthless hound he was, too," commented Tucker.

Again the listener smiled.

Nothing is right about an enemy, he had learned long ago, and with pleasant contempt he looked down on the face of the big man.

"He knew that you needed money, that you had debts."

"I had some debts. I had land and cattle for 'em, too!"

"Stolen money would pay 'em off as well as the land and the cows, and you'd miss that kind of money less. That's what you used, after all!"

"Not then. I wasn't such a fool. I sold cows. But the next season, I bought back twice as many!"

Tucker laughed, gleefully. "I covered my steps all the way. That's what I did."

"This is the idea of Barry Home," said London. "He thinks that you needed the coin, and that you planned the robbery, and put it through. Then you framed him, when you heard that the search was for the trail of a horse with a barred shoe on the left forefoot. That would bring the hunt pretty close to you, perhaps. You took no chances. You sprang the story to the sheriff. You talked about looking out the window and seeing him ride in. Then you planted the loot in his room."

"Well," said Tucker, "he was bright enough to guess part of it, anyway!"

"Yes, he was bright enough. He's no fool. That's one of the things I wanted to tell you."

"Well, when was any Barry Home ever a fool, when it came to making trouble for their betters?'' said Tucker, with a snarl. "Is that all he said?'' he added.

"No. The most important part is coming.''

"What is it?''

"He told me that he wanted to give everybody a fair warning. He warned me, because he said that he once suspected me. He'll warn you before the evening's over.''

"Of what?''

"That this is a death trail. He's going to kill the man who sent him to the pen. He's sworn to do it. He told me that of his own free will.''

"He wouldn't tell you that; he wouldn't put a rope around his neck, in case he—he managed something,'' muttered Tucker.

"You never spent three years in prison. It makes a little difference in the way a man does his thinking and his acting. If he can kill you, Tucker, he'll die happy.''

"And let you out, eh?'' said the rancher.

"Never fear. I'm standing by you, man!'' said London.

"I think you are,'' said Tucker, gloomily. "You're standing by me. What's my interest is yours, in this play of the cards.''

"But you were paid for your work,'' said London. "You held me up for half of the whole loot!''

"Held you up? Wasn't I taking half the risk, then, by covering you up?''

His voice rose high in the argument. "You took your half of the risk after the stage was robbed,'' assented Tom London. "But that's over and done with. I don't talk about spilled milk.''

"Anyway,'' said Tucker, "I never cashed in on my whole half.''

"Why not?''

"There was the diamond stickpin, and the woman's necklace, the pearl one with the diamond clasp. I didn't know how to sell 'em. If I went to a pawnbroker, he'd cheat me. Besides the things were pretty well advertised through the papers, d'ye see? If I tried to get rid of 'em, I might be spotted. And then the goose would be cooked.''

"So you still have 'em?"

"Yeah. I still have 'em. Five thousand dollars' worth of stuff, and more, according to what the papers printed about the missin' articles.''

"Where do you keep 'em, Rance? In the bank?"

"You'd like to know, eh?" asked Tucker, sneering. "But I don't keep 'em in the bank. Never mind where I do keep 'em. No man could find where I've put 'em, and yet—"

He broke off with a laugh of triumph. "And yet," he said, "it's an easy thing to find 'em, too, for a man that knows!''

He laughed again. "All right," said London. "I'm not planning to rob you, Rance. I don't go after small things like that. It's not my game.''

"Five thousand bucks is small to you, eh?"

"Yes. And now, about young Home.''

"That's what I wanta talk about. If he's on a blood trail—and I would've guessed it before—are we to let him run with his nose to the ground till he finds something out?''

"No," said London. "We're not! We stop him.''

"When?"

"Tonight!''

"With what?" said Tucker.

"With a bullet through the brain," said Tom London.

CHAPTER 10
The Moving Hay

TUCKER SHOWED NOT THE LEAST EMOTION, WHEN HE heard this announcement. He merely began to nod and to frown. At last he said: "In the hotel, eh?"

"Why not?"

"That's as good a place as any," said Tucker. "But it's kind of clumsy. I mean, there's so many chances of other folks hearing and seeing."

"The hotel is the best place in the world for me," said the robber. "I've worked it before, Rance, as you ought to guess. I know every corner and nook of it, and I have a few pass-keys that will open every door in the place, and not a sound made!"

He made a gesture of confidence, as though the matter were already accomplished.

"Nothing could be better for me!" said Tom London. "No matter where he may sleep in the hotel tonight, I can open the door for you, Rance!"

"Open the door for me? Open the door for yourself!" exclaimed Tucker. "Why should I do the job?"

"Because he's after you."

"Bah," snorted Tucker. "He'll be after you, too, before he's done. It's your job as much as mine. It's more your job, in fact."

"Why?"

"Robbing and killing is your business," said the rancher.

"It's yours when you need it; you can rob and kill in a pinch as well as anybody, Rance," said Tom London, angrily.

"Can I?"

"Look, man, look," protested London. "I know all about you. I know everything that you've done. I had to find out everything. And I have found you out. I had to have a hold on you, in case of a pinch. Well, Rance, you know what you've done in the past."

"What have I done?" asked Rance Tucker, half sullenly, half defiantly.

"D'you want me to go all through the yarn of what happened to young Barnefeld?" asked London.

The rancher was silent, staring, and again his jaw thrust out, but he did not speak.

"It's all right," said London. "How you got your start in life doesn't make any difference to me. Not a bit! It might interest other folks, but not me, so long as you play fair and square with me, Rance, and never are tempted to turn State's evidence, say, or some little trick like that."

"I'm not that kind of a sneakin' hound," declared Rance.

"Of course, you're not," replied London, "but I don't want you to change. And I suppose this is the reason why I'm no fitter than you are to do the job on that young fellow tonight."

"Listen. I'd like to know how you found out about Barnefeld," muttered Tucker. "And that's not admitting that I had any hand in it."

"Nobody would have thought of looking up that

old story," said London. "Nobody except those that already knew you had stepped a little on the shady side of the law. I knew that already, so I looked back and found out fast enough that, just after Barnefeld was robbed and murdered, Mr. Rance Tucker began to look about for a small piece of land to buy. Then I got on the trail and went to the shack that's still standing at the corner of the Berryville Trail and Chester Road, and down in the cellar I found—"

"Wait a minute!" said Rance Tucker, huskily.

"All right," said London. "I don't want to talk about it, either. Looking at that by match light, in the middle of a howling night as bad as this, made my blood curdle, all right. I don't want to talk about what you've done in the past. But I want to point out that you qualify for this job tonight as well as I do."

Tucker answered: "You've kept your hand in, London. You're surer than me with a gun and, from your own account, him that tackles Barry Home, he'd better be doggone sure with his weapons."

"True," said London. "The best answer is, we open that door and go inside together. I'm going to take my revolvers, Rance. I'll carry the lantern in one hand, and you can get the riot gun out of the store. No, I'll steal that for you as a starter, to show that my heart's in the right place."

"How'll we cover the thing up?" asked Tucker. "We're sure to be suspected. Everybody knows that he hates us and, therefore, that we're sorry that he came back from jail. Everybody will have a look at us, as soon as the body's found!"

"Rance," said Tom London, "suppose that there's a mountain lion running at your heels and a wolf pack away off in the distance. Do you hesitate about killing the mountain lion because you don't know how you'll handle the wolves afterward?"

Tucker shrugged his shoulders.

"Besides," said Tom London, "I have ideas of how we'll be able to dodge, when people come hunting for us. It's the little matter of establishing an alibi, and I'm an expert in that line, Rance."

He laughed, exulting.

"No matter what the other evidence might be," said London, pursuing what was apparently a favorite subject, "no matter if the prints of the murderer's feet go in blood from the dead man to your own parlor rug, and your thumbprints are on the throat of the corpse, and your knife is found in the side of the man who's dead—no matter if all of those things are standing out against you, it makes no difference if you have old man alibi standing beside you, when the sheriff with his posse knocks at the front door."

He broke off and laughed again. "I've alibied myself myself out of a dozen hangings and twenty lifetimes in jail," he concluded, "and I know how I can alibi myself out of this trouble, too."

"And me?"

"Yes, you, too. Look here, Tucker, you don't think that I'm the sort who lets down a partner, do you?"

At this, the vicious element in Tucker became only too evident.

"I'll tell you what I'll expect out of you," said the rancher, "and that is everything that saves your neck and lines your pocket. That's all I expect, and it's each man for himself, as soon as this damned Barry Home is dead. Trust myself in your hands and to your alibis? I'm not such a fool!"

"Good," answered Tom London calmly.

And in the quiet nodding of his head it seemed to Barry Home that he was seeing the most dangerous quality that a criminal can possess, imperturbable coolness under every circumstance. Long was the road that London could travel in this world!

That conclusion had barely come to Home, when it seemed to him that he was seeing the two men below more easily than before. In fact, his face was now in plain view of them, if they should look up!

Then he was aware that he had been sliding forward and was still moving little by little, gradually, steadily. He was not slipping over the surface of the hay, but the hay itself was in motion, a considerable width of this top layer having been unsettled by his weight.

Softly, rapidly, he began to turn his body to the side, but at the first motion the forward impetus of the hay redoubled. It began to shoot away under him, threatening to cast him straight down into the mangers beneath.

In the hundredth part of a second that remained to him, he chose between two things. One was to make a vast effort to reach the wooden upright which was nearest to him; the other was to try to swing about so that he could at least drop feet downward.

If he fell, there was no doubt as to what London and Rance Tucker would do, no doubt in the world. They would simply thank the fortune that delivered him into their hands and that would be the end of Barry Home!

So he flung himself sidewise toward the upright. The hay shot out from underneath him and went down in a great cloud.

The frightened horses pulled back from their mangers, snorting and squealing as though the sky were falling on their heads, and the voice of London shouted:

"There! Look! It's Home!"

The left hand of Barry Home had missed the

upright entirely. The right had caught hold, however, and, as a gun spoke beneath him and a bullet tore through the hay at his side, he jerked himself back to the safety and darkness at the top of the mow.

Instantly the lantern was extinguished below him. He heard a muttering of voices; the grinding of the wheels of the sliding door on the runway, the whistling of the icy storm through the aperture, and then the heavy slamming of the door.

He was alone in the barn except for the animals. All the information which he had gained was now more than counterbalanced, since his enemies had learned the fullness of his knowledge.

There had been a vast advantage for him, that was now totally relinquished, for they would understand that he had overheard their mutual admissions, their plans for his murder. They would be on guard. If they were dangerous before, they would be doubly dangerous now that they knew that he was forewarned and fully aware of their admitted guilt.

So, lying prone in the hay, Barry Home gritted his teeth together. He had a wild impulse to descend at once, rush to the hotel, borrow or steal a gun, and turn it loose upon the precious pair.

But what was gained if he killed them and, in turn, was hanged for that crime?

For a moment, his brain whirled.

Something had to be done quickly, but the very need of haste paralyzed his wits, and he could accomplish nothing.

At last, he fumbled his way down the edge of the haymow, found the ladder of crosspieces nailed to one of the great uprights, and descended. He would have to find his plans as he walked blindly back toward the hotel.

CHAPTER 11

Into The Storm

WHEN HE REACHED THE HOUSE, HE WENT INTO THE kitchen a moment and found Mrs. Loomis standing at the inner door ringing a great brazen-lipped bell with all her might. She had a happy expression on her face.

Why should the woman be ringing this bell in the middle of the night, unless she were utterly mad?

The he remembered; no matter how much had passed since the coming of twilight and that moment when he first saw Loomis in the distance, the actual time that had passed had been very short, and the meal, which was in course of preparation on his arrival, was now merely ready for the table. It was the supper bell which Mrs. Loomis was sounding!

Patty came swiftly to him and touched his hand. "What's the matter, Barry?" she asked him. "And what have you done?"

He looked down at himself. He had not been too abstracted on the way from the barn to neglect the obvious precaution of brushing off the hay that stuck to him. There was no sign of it on his clothes, whatever she saw was in his face, and certainly in his heart there was murder to match whatever she could guess.

"You have a horse, Patty, haven't you?"

"I have one," she said.

He looked down and saw that her eyes were troubled as she searched his face again.

"I want to borrow it," he said. "Which is it?"

"The blue roan gelding on the near side of the barn," said Patty Loomis. "What—"

She did not complete her question.

"It's all right, Patty," he said.

He nodded to reassure her and saw that far more than a mere gesture was needed to make her happy about him. A lump rippled up in her throat and fell again.

"I suppose it's all right," she said. "But you're going to stop and take some supper before you leave?"

"No supper. I have to ride three pretty brisk miles, and ride 'em now."

"You'll be back before long?"

"I'll be back before very long. Good-by, Patty."

He glanced uneasily around the kitchen as he spoke.

"You want something else?" she asked.

"Yes, but—"

"You want a gun?" said the girl.

He flushed, and then set his teeth.

"I want a gun," he murmured.

She was off in a flash, gesturing toward the side door. There in the hall he waited, and she came to him with her hand beneath her apron; when she took it out, she was carrying a long, heavy-barreled single-action Colt.

"The kind you like," she said.

He handled it fondly. At the touch of his fingers

on the roughened grip, confidence ran warmly through his body, and that unforgotten delight of battle wiped out all fear of consequences. No man in the world could be trusted, perhaps, but this was a friend that would not fail him.

Then he saw the girl, so pale with fear that her eyes seemed darker, and he wondered at her.

"It's in good shape," said Barry Home. "I see it's loaded and clean and well oiled."

"Yes, it is," she answered, the haunted look never leaving her.

"By thunder," said Barry Home, suddenly, "if it weren't for the solemn oath I've made, I wouldn't leave you now, Pat. I'd stay here with you, and never raise my hand in my whole life except to make you happy."

A pitiful smile plucked at her lips and was gone again. She nodded.

"Yes, Barry," said she.

"It's your father's gun?" he added.

"Yes," she whispered, overcome with emotion against which she kept on fighting.

He closed his eyes and saw again, for a moment, the picture of Hal Loomis, the brother of Dave, but very different from the hotel keeper was that big, burly, adventurous man who had trekked from the deserts of South Africa to the snows of Alaska, hunting for gold, laboring with the strength of a giant to find treasure for his family, and never succeeding, but getting instead, a long series of hard knocks. Fate had never daunted him with her hard strokes, however, and to the end he had fought hard and cleanly.

It was the gun of Hal Loomis, now, that he gripped in his right hand. And it seemed to Barry Home that the ghost of the dead man stood with a troubled face behind his daughter and looked sadly, reproachfully at him above her head.

Home thrust the gun inside his coat. "It's going to come out right!" he declared.

"Yes," she murmured, and again she nodded and again the wave of apprehension widened and darkened her eyes.

He put a hand on either side of her face and stood close while an agony of tenderness wrenched at his heart.

"You wait, Pat," he said. "The time's coming when I'll be able to show what you mean to me. You've given me a horse and a gun tonight, and I'll promise you this, I'll use 'em for no wrong thing. I'll never shoot till it's my life or another man's."

"Good old Barry," said she, and smiled again at him in a way that made the tears rush into his eyes.

He had to hurry out from the house, breathing deep and hard to restore his self-confidence and remove the aching pity from his heart.

Then he was in the barn again, lighting the lantern which swung a little back and forth on its wooden peg near the door. Of course, it was the pressure of a draft that moved it, but it was to Barry Home exactly as though the hand of Tom London had that very instant hung it in place.

By the lantern light, he looked up grimly toward the place where he had lain stretched out on the top of the mow. Looking down, it had seemed to him that he had been at a very secure distance. A neck-breaking distance, almost certainly. Looking up, however, it seemed that Tom London could not possibly have missed his shot.

There was the beam he had reached and by which he had managed to snatch himself back to safety and darkness; and down on top of the manger he saw lying the spilled mass of the fallen hay, with two horses working happily away on it.

The blue roan was one of them, a mustang built long and low, with plenty of driving power in his quarters and a fine, muscular slope to his shoulders. He was not a pretty horse, but one that looked serviceable, such a horse as one would expect the daughter of big Hal Loomis to select for herself.

He got the saddle off the peg on the wall, and the blue roan tried to kick it out of his hands. That did not either alarm or annoy him, but brought a grin to his lips.

He could almost have told her horse by the manner of the beast. She was always selecting the worst-mannered horse in the whole herd, then gradually reforming it until it became as wise and gentle as a household pet. She had been doing it with one horse after another from the days of her childhood, and there was another instance.

As he finally got the saddle in place and wedged the bit at last between the angry teeth of the gelding, he told himself that nowhere in the world could another girl be found like Patty Loomis, a perfect mate for him. There was nothing under heaven that he would not do for her—nothing except to give up the vow which he had made long ago in the solitude of his cell.

That was what he told himself, fiercely, and softly moved his lips. All the while it was as though she were standing at his shoulder, silently, as she had stood before him in the hall, grieving with all her heart at whatever terrible danger he was intending to face, but loyally helping him to the extent of her ability. Aye, there was a woman for him or for any man!

He gave the cinches another tug, put out the lantern, and led the mustang to the barn door.

The gleam of that lantern might well have been seen at the hotel and if Tom London or the rancher, Tucker, noticed the light, either one of them or both might be waiting now outside the barn. He hesitated, thinking of this, before he pulled back the sliding door.

When he thought of all that lay before him in the bitter cold of this night and its darkness, he realized, if he kept pausing for every possible thought of danger, he would never get through to the morning, he would never be able to execute any of his plans.

So he thrust the door boldly open.

The blue roan grunted and pulled back, as the wind knifed into it. A tarpaulin hanging near the door flapped loudly in the rush of the air.

The sliding fingers of the cold pried under the ribs of Barry Home and got at the pit of his stomach. Brave man or coward, no one could face such whip-driven cold as this without something more than the apparel he was wearing! The snow was coming faster, riding the wind with a scream and cutting the skin of his face as it struck him.

It was such a night as to make one wonder what, other than raving idiocy, would make any man leave shelter for the open. But Barry Home did not hesitate. Only, first, he took the tarpaulin hanging beside the door and tied it around his shoulders.

Then he led the mustang out, closed the door, mounted, and left the corral for the open road.

The wind, in the meantime, gathered force and leaped on him with a yell, when he had gone through the corral gate. Through the tarpaulin and through his own wretchedly insufficient clothes, the chill of the storm soaked like water through paper.

He gave himself some comfort by remembering what he had read of the gigantic Patagonians, who endure a weather that is continual storm and ice in nakedness, with only one bit of leather, like a shield, strapped to their bodies and turned toward the prevailing wind.

He was better than that, at least, in his equipment, as he started riding through the blizzard for the house of Rance Tucker.

CHAPTER 12
At The Window

THE WIND HAD SHIFTED SO THAT IT BEAT STRAIGHT IN his face all the way to the Tucker house. It was increasing in force until, in the throat of the pass, it came at him with such violence it threatened to lift him out of the saddle. It seemed wonderful to him that anything so cold could have such buoyancy.

How the mustang managed to keep going was a mystery to the rider. He flattened himself along the neck of the strong-hearted gelding and kicked it in the ribs, now and then, by way of encouragement, and at every kick the horse shook his head and freshened his trot.

A trot was all that could be managed with safety, now that the road was wet and frozen underfoot, and doubly treacherous where the snow had drifted across it in the hollows. Sometimes, as they went on, the wind scooped up a cloud of the fallen snow and sent it with hurricane swiftness like a great flying, ghostly mist into the face of Barry.

Had it not been for the tarpaulin that covered his shoulders and the upper part of his body, he knew that he would have had to give up the journey before he had covered the first half mile. Even as it was, when the first mile had ended, he was certain that he would be a dead man before he went over the next two.

But he could remember other miseries of cold almost as great. Every winter there were sure to be a few occasions when a rider would be forced to venture his very life for the sake of the cattle on the range. So he was well inured to this exposure; moreover, experience hardens the mind.

The second mile brought him into the pass itself, where his courage failed him for a moment. Perhaps, he would have turned back, after all, except that the blue roan, shaking its ugly head, bored resolutely on into the teeth of the storm. That roused his heart with admiration for the poor beast that could have no understanding of the purpose for which this adventure was undertaken, which was supported and urged along merely by the will of the rider and perhaps by a somewhat perverse determination to conquer every obstacle that could be presented.

Out of the pass, the country widened into rolling hills, and the wind, no longer compressed in a funnel, raged less furiously. He was able to sit up straight on the horse and he began to swing his arms to quicken the circulation as he came to the house of Rance Tucker, lying long and low, a big, black hulk.

All was familiar ground to him here. He had worked long enough for the thrifty rancher to have a map of the layout printed in his mind. It would be useful to him, now.

In the first place, he had to cache his horse.

He went behind the woodshed where it abutted on the smokehouse, where the hundreds of hams and sides of bacon were cured every year by Rance Tucker, who raised his own pigs to feed his own crew, and had something left over to sell cheaply to the Loomis store. The junction of the two sheds formed a perfect windbreak, and when the rider threw the reins, the blue roan cuddled up contentedly into the angle thus formed, as though this were exactly the sort of stabling it was used to.

That was sufficient shelter, at least, to keep the tough brute from any danger of freezing.

Barry Home remained there beside the horse for a moment, jumping up and down and thrashing his arms about against his body until he was in a glow. He waited with his eyes closed, also, until the wind-strain was gone out of them. He practiced passing the revolver out of his coat and back inside it a score of times, to make sure that he was familiar with the lie of the weapon.

When he was ready, he wiped his eyes, settled his hat firmly on his head, and then turned the corner of the smokehouse into the screech of the gale again.

A moment later he was beside the leeward wall of the house, with only the howling of the wind overhead, as it shot across the roof of the house and sped away, sloping rapidly down to the ground again. Here, there was no snow upon the ground, and he could give thanks for that, because it would be easy for his feet to grow numb while he waited out here, slowly exploring.

He tried the light in the kitchen, first. Rubbing away a frost of cold mist in a lower corner of a pane, he looked through the spy hole and saw the whole room easily, while the white frosting secured him from discovery.

Mrs. Tucker was there at the sink, a tall and bony woman with what seemed a curving rod down her back but what was in reality her spinal column, sticking out from the starving flesh.

It was said that Mrs. Tucker was not in the habit of cooking for herself when her menfolk were out of the house. She fed them well enough when they were present but, for her own part, a glass of milk and a few crackers were enough to suit her, or the trimmings of meat left on a leg of mutton after most of the carving had been completed.

On bits and scraps she was pleased to maintain herself when she was alone, and well could Barry Home remember the starved and forbidding eye with which she followed the trencher work of the men at her table while she sat erect at one end with her mouth pinched into a straight line and the devil in her glances.

She was not, in fact, washing up dishes after her supper. She was busily scrubbing at the sink, but through the window he could see that she was using the empty evening to rub up all of the kitchen pots and pans. With her sleeves rolled up to the elbows, she attacked the pots with a huge rattling, scrubbing at them with a brush and sand, first, and then polishing them off to shining dryness.

Well, there were certain virtues in such a woman, Barry Home supposed. But he did not wish to find them again in any woman he married, any mother of sons of his. It seemed to him that the evil that had spread abroad through that house had almost entirely sprung out of her. Evil she was, and to evil she gave birth!

As he watched, the door was flung open, and young Tucker came striding into the kitchen. Not a sound did his footfall make on the floor, so loud was the shouting of the storm outside, in the ears of the watcher, and he heard not a whisper of the loud cry of Mrs. Tucker though he could see the opening of her mouth and the straining of her lips as she ran toward her son. Black was the face of

Lew Tucker and solemn his look. What would he tell his mother?

Barry shrugged his shoulders and shook his head. Whatever else might happen that night, it was plain that Lew Tucker had received a frightful blow to his pride; otherwise, he would not have shrunk from his father in time of need.

Why had he lingered on the way? What had he been doing? Well, perhaps he had been sitting in the darkness of the barn, after unsaddling his horse, holding his head between his hands, in thought, pondering his downfall and his shame.

There was some pity in the heart of Barry Home as he turned from the kitchen window and walked up the side of the house to the next lighted window, which opened out from the living room.

Somewhere in that house were the articles of the loot which the rancher had named to his partner, Tom London. If he could find them, Barry Home could reverse the judgment against himself and thus punishment would fall where it had been so long and so richly merited.

Where was he to search? He had gathered from the story of the rancher that the stuff was hidden, at least in part, in some open and obvious place, where the eye was not likely to recognize it. Otherwise, Rance Tucker would not have laughed with such exultation. Furthermore, his assurance must have been absolute, or he would never have confided so much to Tom London. But still there was hope in young Barry Home that he might be able to penetrate to the heart of the mystery.

He looked through the living room window as he had looked through the kitchen window and saw it not too brightly illuminated by the lamp with the circular burner which was suspended above the little round center table, the light made more brilliant by strands of clouded glass beads that hung from a circular frame all around the lamp.

Beneath that glow he saw the books and could name them—the velvet-covered, brass-studded album of family portraits, *Pilgrim's Progress*, the book of the flowers of the wayside and the field, and the battered, ancient dictionary which, so far as he could remember, had never been opened except to look up populations that had been outgrown twenty years before.

He grinned sourly as he surveyed the rest of the room, the empty fireplace—in spite of this weather!—and the stiff-backed chairs with moth-eaten plush covering the seats.

There had been no happiness during the months he had worked for the Tuckers, only the satisfaction of holding down a place where few cowpunchers would stay more than a few weeks at a time, underfed and underpaid.

He tried the window with his hand. It seemed fast, at first, but then it shuddered and finally rose a little.

It must not be allowed to make a sound that would be audible at the farther end of the house.

He was about to push it up a sufficient distance to enable him to climb inside, when something made him turn his head, and now he saw three riders coming rapidly down the road from the pass.

He must not be seen against the lighted square of the window, so he crouched down close to the ground, and saw the riders swing in through the gate to the Tucker house.

One of them was surely Rance Tucker!

The heart of the young fellow quickened. If ever a man sensed the near approach of fate, it was Barry, as he saw the three shadows proceed to the barn, dismount, and pass into the darkness of that building.

CHAPTER 13
The Glass Fringe

He was in a quandary, once the three had disappeared, and a light gleamed inside the barn from a lantern. He might slip out to the barn and try to overhear what was passing there, as he had spied on London and Tucker.

But probably they were coming straight back toward the house. And he might do something with them now. If he recognized them in time, he could shout a challenge and open fire; on London and Tucker, yes, and perhaps he could kill them both; but the third man? That complicated everything.

Besides, even if the third man had not been there, it was no good, this shooting business. If anything happened to London and Tucker, the blame would be attributed to him as directly as though a thousand pairs of eyes had seen him do the shooting.

What was his triumph of revenge, then, if he passed from freedom back to prison, and from prison to the hangman's rope?

Savagely he brooded as he crouched in the cold and saw the door of the barn open again.

Out came the trio. The barn was dark again behind them. There came a pause in the storm's uproar and distinctly he heard the rumbling of the wheels of the sliding door on the runway.

As the three came closer, he recognized two of them. The larger man was Rance Tucker, he was certain, and even more unmistakable was Tom London from a certain grace of carriage which he retained even when leaning against the wind.

Slowly they came on, slowing almost to a halt, from time to time, as the force of the storm staggered them. They came very close and, staring hard, straining his eyes, the young fellow made sure of the third man. It was the sheriff!

Barry set his teeth, for the thing became clear. Tucker and London when they knew that they were overheard, had made up their minds that they were in immediate danger of their lives. They had cooked up some sort of a story to interest the sheriff, and now they were gathered together to watch out this night in safety; this night, at least, under the broad shield of the law. All Barry's difficulties from that moment were doubled and redoubled!

They entered the house. Presently they came into the living room. In the entrance hall, they had taken off their coats. But their faces were blue and red with cold, and they began to stamp and strike their bodies with their hands.

Tucker made angry gestures toward the empty hearth. His son came in; everyone was speaking. Mrs. Tucker appeared, her ugly face illumined as she embraced her husband on his safe return. Then the party trooped through the farther door, evidently going in to take advantage of the warmth that the kitchen stove would offer to them.

Rance remained a pace behind the others. As

they disappeared through the doorway the watcher at the frosted window saw through his peephole how the rancher paused, swept his big hand through the strands of the glass beads around the hanging lamp; then, with a sly smile of content, followed the others.

The watcher shook his head.

He had a vast sense of defeat. With four men inside that house, all armed, all undoubtedly on the lookout to ward off danger directly threatening them from him, there seemed nothing left but to get his horse and return to Loomis, with the single advantage that the storm would then be blowing at his back.

And then he knew that he could not return. He could not leave these detested enemies any more than a starving wolf can leave the trail of a bull moose, though it knows that it is far too weak to pull down the prize when it has been brought to bay.

So he lingered there, shuddering with the cold, trying to think. He could form no plan. But somewhere in the house there was the proof that would shift blame from his shoulders to those of Rance Tucker. He must find it. He could not trace it if he remained there in the outer night. No, he must enter.

After he was inside, inspiration might come to him, he felt, so he rounded to the front of the house, tried the door, found it unlatched, and entered quickly, sliding through a narrow aperture and shutting the door behind him again.

Even so, he heard the whoop of the wind go with a hollow and a whistling sound through the house. Would that alarm the inmates of the place?

A noise of voices arose suddenly from the back of the house. He recognized the heavy tones of Lew Tucker, saying: "The front door was opened, then. I know the way the wind come in."

The door to the kitchen was ajar. Lew Tucker stood in the gap of it, frowning, and looking across the living room toward the darkness of the hallway.

"Don't be a fool, Lew," said the voice of Rance Tucker. "That was the howl of the wind comin' down the chimney. I seen the smoke and ashes puff out of the stove."

"Somebody opened the front door!" insisted Lew.

"Well, go and see, then," urged his father, carelessly. "You ain't gonna take my word for it, so you go and make up your mind for yourself, will you?"

"Yes, I will," growled Lew.

And he drew out a big Colt to assist him in the search! Barry Home shrank back against the wall, rolling his eyes wildly from side to side. There was no other door opening into the hallway, he knew, except that of the living room. Where could he hide himself, then?

There were only the long, dripping overcoats and slickers that hung against the wall, but for a good reason he would not use that refuge.

Lew Tucker, in the meantime, was striding straight on.

Barry Home groaned, his throat swelling and aching with the suppression of the sound. It was not young Lew Tucker that he wanted. It was the father of that young fellow! But there was Lew coming, armed, and with a resolved face!

Home slid back into the darkest corner, and there he squatted on his heels against the wall. Chance would have to help him now. As for his own revolver, he drew it with a numb, cold hand, and held its muzzle down, beside his knee.

Then Tucker stood in the door and moved his head, staring about him, gun held at the raised ready position for firing. Plainly he meant business of the most serious kind.

He stepped forward. Exactly as Barry Home had expected, he brushed aside the wet overcoats, found nothing, and finally with a shake of the head turned away. He reached the doorway, jerked his head sidewise, and looked straight at the spot where Home was crouched.

A thousandth part of a second was Lew Tucker from death, at that instant; then he went on slowly; and Barry Home was blinded by a rush of blood to the head, and staggered by the pounding of the pulse in his temple.

He stood up, trembling, and breathing deeply; he heard the kitchen door opening again and the sound of voices rolling out toward him.

"Well, Lew?" asked Rance.

"I guess I was wrong. If that door was opened, it was closed without anybody coming inside."

"You look in the hall?"

"Yes."

"Nothin' anywhere?"

"No, not a soul," said Lew Tucker, and closed the door on his own last words.

Barry Home smiled as he listened, and then glided into the living room.

He glanced at the empty hearth, not that he expected to see the warmth of a fire flickering there, but because everyone else had looked in that direction on entering the room. He had no instant to waste on odd details by glancing here and there, but he made sure of the emptiness of the hearth first of all, gritting his teeth at his own folly at the same moment.

Then he stood under the flare of the lamp. How perfect a target he was for anyone who opened the door of the kitchen at that moment! Then he did as he had seen Rance Tucker do. He drew out the bead fringe that dangled around the lamp!

What was the meaning of that caressing gesture on the part of the rancher? What was the meaning of the sly and exulting smile of the man?

He could find no reason for that either and, leaving the string of glass beads to clash softly together as he stepped back, he removed himself a pace and looked uncertainly toward the door of the kitchen. Out of the other room came the steady rumble of men's voices, with the shrill overtone of Mrs. Tucker cutting through with an opinion, now and again.

There was reason for him to tremble. Though he did not actually shake, every nerve in his body was painfully on the alert, reaching out, probing on all sides toward possible danger. That right hand of his, now recovering from the cold, tingling and throbbing with heat, was eager to snatch out his revolver.

One gun against four, that was not an easy game, even for a Barry Home fighting for his life!

He could see, now, that when he examined the beaded fringe under the lamp, he was not in exactly the same spot where Rance Tucker had stood.

He moved to the same place, thrust out his hand, and placed it under the dangling strings of glass beads.

Even then he would not have found a difference if his eyes had not been sharpened by keen necessity. As it was, however, he could see that whereas the other strings turned dark and cold in the shadow of his hand, one of them appeared faintly luminous, and of a softer, creamier texture of light.

They were not glass at all! They were pearls!

CHAPTER 14
Sparks

HE GLANCED UP FROM THEM, SUDDENLY, TO THE larger bit of cut glass from which the particular string of beads dangled and saw that it was a good bit smaller than the other pieces of glass around the lamp, the headpieces from which the strings dangled. It was cut in many more facets, and it cast out a spark of fire, instead of the duller flash of the other bits.

It was not glass any more than the string of beads beneath it. It was the same valuable stick-pin diamond!

No wonder that Rance Tucker had said that he had hidden the little treasures where no man could find them, though they were easy enough to locate, when one only knew the key!

He himself might have searched through the house forever, and vainly, except that he had chanced to be on hand to see the gesture of Tucker. But now he knew, and he reached up his hand to strip away the prize.

He checked himself. It was not the possession

of that thing that he really wanted. A few thousand dollars mattered nothing, as a matter of fact. What was important was that while this string dangled here, it was proclaiming with every flash, with every gleam of jeweled light, that Rance Tucker had a share, at least, in the robbery of the stagecoach to Crystal Creek.

No, the value of the evidence lay simply in the place where it hung on view, if he could bring the eyes of authority to glance at it.

It meant, in a single flash, the removal from his own shoulders of all implication in the crime for which he had suffered for three years. It meant his reestablishment as a respectable citizen.

Respectable citizen?

His upper lip twitched with disdainful scorn as he thought of the phrase. He knew, he thought, what respectability amounted to now. As he had told the girl, it was merely the ability to hide the evidences of crime. So London and Tucker had done. For three years they had continued being respectable, while he, poor fool, suffered every pang short of damnation.

Breathing deep, he stared at the little string of pearls and the diamond above them. How simple it was; how clever! He almost stopped hating Rance Tucker, in his admiration for this stroke of cleverness.

A shot that shattered a pane of glass in the window through which he himself had looked, not long before, cut short these speculations.

He felt the whir of the bullet past his face and then turned and dived for cover.

Not toward the hall door, for that was too far away, but just to the left of the living room fireplace there was another doorway that opened on the stairs that led to the second story.

At that door he aimed himself, like a projectile, running low, his shoulder bunched and the muscles hardened. He struck the door. It crashed before him as the second and third bullets plunged into the woodwork that framed him. And forward he pitched onto the broad lower steps of the stairway. In his ears was the yelling voice of Rance Tucker, from outside the house: "I got him! I nailed him! I nailed him! Run him down, damn him! I got Barry Home!"

People were coming with a rush from the kitchen, as Home, more than half stunned, picked himself up and staggered up the stairs.

He got to the first landing, where the steps turned and wound upward at a new angle, before the people from the kitchen rushed in and reached the broken door that he had battered down.

He turned and fired, not at them, but above their heads, and heard the shriek of Mrs. Tucker.

He was still bewildered by the shock he had received so that as he ran on up the steps to the hall above, he could only vaguely hear the clamor of the voices and wonder if the bullet by any chance had actually struck poor Mrs. Tucker.

Then he was in the hall above.

They were not following. He stood still, in the cold, clammy darkness, and listened to their voices.

Rance Tucker was already in the room, shouting in triumph.

"The third shot, I nailed him. I split his back open for him. He's a dead rat. I nailed him fair between the shoulders!"

There was so much confidence in his voice that Barry Home actually slid his left hand up behind his back toward the shoulder blades, and he started as his fingers touched moisture.

No, of course, that was simply melted snow. And Rance Tucker was enjoying the same illusion that hunters have, when they swear they have seen half a dozen bullets strike the bear; and yet bruin is scampering rapidly away through the brush, unscathed.

"I don't see any blood," said the voice of the sheriff.

"There mightn't be any blood on the floor, but there's blood oozing down his clothes and his body. There's blood being pumped right out from his heart this minute, red blood, lifeblood!" shouted Rance Tucker. "Tom, he ain't gonna bother us no more!"

"I hope you're right," said London.

"Right? You hope I'm right? I know I'm right. I don't seem such a fool now, do I, comin' out from the kitchen into the cold again? No, I got an instinct. I can tell when things are goin' wrong!"

"He'll get out of the house and away," said the sheriff.

"He'll die before he gets fifty steps," said Rance Tucker, filled with confidence.

"We've gotta keep watch. There's a moon blowed up over the mountains, now, and it gives plenty of light," said Lew Tucker. "We gotta go and lie out and wait, some of us!"

"You'll be freezing yourselves to death, you crazy things," said Mrs. Tucker.

"Lew is right," broke in the sheriff. "We can't take any chances. If it's Barry Home, and if he's in this house, he means to fight his way out, unless your bullet got him, poor young fool!"

"Poor young murderer, you mean!" said Mrs. Tucker. "The bloodthirsty young scoundrel. I hope—"

What she hoped remained unknown.

For now the sheriff broke in with a crisp, clear voice: "Rance, you and Lew and Tom London get outside and watch the house. Stay there for an hour. You'll have moonlight to do it. Use shotguns. Shoot at any shadow that tries to get free from the place. Understand?"

"I understand," said Rance Tucker. "But you won't need to wait for a whole hour. He's running blood, I tell you. His blood is soaking through the flooring, someplace in the house. I split his wishbone, boys. I was kind of unsteady, seeing him first, but the third shot, I nailed him. I seen him go crash when he hit the door."

He laughed in his exultation.

The voice of the sheriff cut in again: "Get out there on the double. Every Barry Home is a tough man. It's hard to kill a Barry Home with one bullet. Get out there, now, and look things over. Be sharp, too. He's gonna slide through your fingers, if you don't look out. If it's only to drag himself away and die in some hole or corner where he'll never be found. If you wanta find your dead man, get outside. I'll hold things down in here. Before you're froze to death, one of you come back in. Rance, you're the oldest. You come back inside after an hour, and I'll go out and take your place. We're gonna have to keep a watch on the outside of the house all night. When the morning comes, we'll start in searchin' for the body."

"It's a waste of time," said Rance Tucker. "I split his wishbone for him, I tell you."

"Go and do what you're told to do by somebody that knows!" said Mrs. Tucker. "Don't go and dispute with the sheriff, Rance!"

"Come on, Pa," urged the son.

"Oh, I'll go," said Rance Tucker. "Only, it's a big night for me. A big night when I've bagged Barry Home, and don't you forget it!"

"All right, Rance," said Tom London, who spoke very little at this moment. "The main thing is for us to keep from freezing while we're out there in the open. We'll need all the coats and slickers that you have in the house."

"They're in the hall, stacks of 'em," said Mrs. Tucker. "And I'll fire up in the kitchen stove and get some coffee to boiling for you boys. I'll fetch it out to you. There ain't no more comfort than hot coffee in the cold."

"Make it good and strong, Ma," said Lew Tucker. "Not that dishwater that you're likely to serve up!"

"Only," said Mrs. Tucker, "are you sure that that murderer ain't gonna come down from upstairs and break in on us? Are you sure that you hurt him bad enough to take the fight out of him?"

"Him?" said Rance Tucker. "You take my word for it. He's lying on his face dead, somewhere up in the hall. That's all. He's dead, right now. But I guess we'd better play safe, like the sheriff says. That's the best way. Always the best way, to play safe when you're up against a Barry Home!"

He laughed again, at the end of this speech, as though he had said something very witty.

It was mere excess of joy and animal spirits that brought the merriment forth.

Then, standing frozen to his place in the upper hall, Barry Home heard their muffled voices as they got into coats and slickers, then heard them stamping through the door. He did not attempt to get through a second-story window to the ground. That would be difficult and dangerous business, while the outer walls of the house were iced over with sleet. For his own part, he had formed another and what seemed to him a much better plan.

Mrs. Tucker was already in the kitchen, to judge by the rattling of iron, which seemed to indicate that she had opened up the stove and was loading it with wood again.

She would soon have the coffeepot on, steaming

and boiling. In the meantime, the front door slammed heavily, the weight of the wind hurling it shut with a crash, while the breath of the storm whistled and screamed through the house.

Barry Home took advantage of that uproar to make, rapidly, the first three steps of the descent down the stairs.

CHAPTER 15
A Slow Descent

THE LIVING ROOM WAS, UNDOUBTEDLY, THE CRUCIAL place to hold from a tactical point of view, if one wished to make sure of what happened in the house, and the sheriff was very right in remaining there. Barry Home was glad for almost the same reason for, according to his present plan, it was the sheriff that he wanted to get at.

But he made his descent cautiously. From the living room, there came no sound whatever for a time, and meanwhile he was coming down the stairs, but in such a way that his procedure would have appeared extremely erratic to anyone not initiated.

For he never moved until the wind caught hold of the house and shook it from head to heel with a furious blast. Then he ventured softly down, two or three steps at a time. After this he would pause, motionless, two or three minutes, until another blast of the hurricane descended on the place.

After twenty minutes of these precautions, he got finally to the bottom of the stairs. And now he stood beside the broken door. Inside that bright frame was the room with Sheriff Bert Wayland waiting, gun ready, eyes keen as a hawk's. A formidable man was Bert Wayland, not one to talk a great deal; but he could shoot straight and fast. His record was long; there were many deaths to decorate the length of it.

That was the reason why the young man hesitated long moments until the door of the kitchen opened, and the voice of Mrs. Tucker, husky with excitement, said: "Well, Mr. Wayland, is everything all right?"

"Everything will be all right, so far as the house goes," said the sheriff, "till you hear a gunshot, and I drop dead. I'm watchin' that doorway, yonder. I'm watchin' it as though the devil might stick his head around the corner of it almost any minute."

"Good for you," said Mrs. Tucker, heartily, "because a devil is what he is. I can't understand why the prison should go and turn loose a killer like him. Prisons is the place for 'em, and no place else!"

"Maybe," said the sheriff.

"I'll be fetching you in a cup of coffee, Sheriff Wayland, in a coupla shakes," said Mrs. Tucker, cordially, and slammed the kitchen door.

That instant, surely, the eyes of the sheriff would wander toward the place where his hostess had disappeared. That instant Barry Home glided into the frame of the broken door and leveled his gun, hip-high, and saw the glance of Wayland, as he had expected, swinging back from the kitchen door.

The sheriff was seated in a straight chair, well to the side of the center table, so that the glare from the lamp, shining down, would not trouble his eyes in taking aim. His gun rested on his knees.

But he made no effort to raise it and fire when he saw that he was covered, and by whom.

Many things had been said of Barry Home, first, second, and third, but never had any man suggested that any one of the three failed to shoot straight. The sheriff, at least, cherished no such delusion.

Without moving his gun hand, his head rose as he stiffened a little in the chair and his nostrils flared. He had the attitude of a man steeling himself to receive the frightful shock of a bullet that would strike over his heart and tear its way through his life.

"Lean over and put that gun on the floor," said Barry Home.

The sheriff obeyed.

"Now stand up, turn your back to me, and hoist your hands."

Again the sheriff obeyed.

Barry Home went to him and laid the muzzle of his revolver in the small of the sheriff's back. He nudged it hard against the spine of the helpless man.

"You see where you stand," said Home.

"I've been beat before," said the sheriff. "Only tonight I was a fool to trust Rance Tucker! He split your wishbone, did he?"

He groaned as he spoke.

The left hand of Home went deftly over him. There was not a bulge to indicate another weapon.

"That's all right," said Barry Home. "Now come over here."

He steered the sheriff with a hand on his shoulder until he came to a certain point facing the hanging lamp. Then, stepping forward, he laid the muzzle of his gun against the sheriff's breast.

"You don't need this much light to murder me by, Barry, do you?" asked the sheriff, calmly.

And Barry Home wondered. He had seen men

die, young as he was, and in the prison he had heard many tales of death. Yet there was something both terrible and fine in the calm of the sheriff, who was taking his turn under the muzzle of a gun. How would he, Barry Home, react in a similar situation?

With his left hand, he reached out and fumbled behind the glass strings of beads.

"Look at this, not at my gun," he advised. "There's your answer!"

"I don't see nothin', Barry," said the sheriff, as calmly as ever.

"Look again, at the string that hangs from the cut-glass bit that's smaller than the others. See anything now?"

"Yeah. It's smaller. The beads are bigger, though."

"Reach out and break that off from the frame," ordered Barry Home.

"It's pretty nigh funny enough to make me laugh," said the sheriff, "though I know that I'm gonna catch thunder and lightning in a minute."

"You're wrong," said Barry Home. "You'll see how wrong you are in another minute. But do as I say."

The sheriff obeyed once more and stood gravely, holding the dangling string of beads and the diamond at the top of them in his hand.

"Don't look at me," said Barry Home. "Look at the stuff in your hand."

"I see it," said Wayland.

"Look again. Is that stuff glass."

The sheriff stared, and then started.

"By thunderation!" he muttered, under his breath.

"That stuff," said Barry Home, "was all described by the papers at the time the Crystal Creek stage was robbed. A pearl necklace, and a diamond stickpin. Worth a couple of thousand dollars apiece."

"By thunderation," repeated the amazed sheriff.

"Pull yourself together," said Barry Home. "Tom London and Rance Tucker should have served that prison sentence, not I. You remember that I always swore I had nothing to do with it? London robbed the stage. You remember the horse trail business? London and Tucker framed it together to put the blame on me. Tonight, in the Loomis barn, I heard them talk the whole thing out. The diamond and the pearls, Tucker was afraid to sell for fear he'd be traced through 'em. He had this idea for concealing his stuff, and it's a good idea, I say."

"Good idea? It's a great idea!" said the sheriff. "It—it's a good enough idea for a book. But hold on, Barry. You mean to say that the State was wrong, and you were innocent all the while?"

"That's what I mean."

He quietly put up his gun as he spoke.

"Take your Colt again, Wayland. Call in Rance Tucker. Show him that stuff and ask him where he got it. And watch his face!' "

The sheriff drew in a great breath as he scooped up his gun. For a moment it seemed, from his savage face, as though he intended to turn his bullets upon the young fellow, but what he said was: "The hounds, the dirty hounds! And a poor kid went to prison and hell for 'em, eh? Oh, Barry, I'm a sad man when I think what a fool I've been! A sad man!"

He went to the front door, opened it and, as the wind whistled into the house, his voice was heard calling, faint and far away: "Rance! Oh, Rance Tucker, come in!"

Almost at once Rance Tucker was entering the house, and the whistling of the wind was shut out as the front door closed.

"Wayland, have you got him?" exclaimed Tucker.

Barry had slipped back through the broken door and waited, peering out through the safe mask of shadow. He saw the two come into the room, the face of Tucker eagerly expectant.

Suddenly the sheriff held the string of beads before him.

"Where'd you get this, Tucker?" asked Wayland, sharply.

The jaw of Rance Tucker dropped.

"Damn you!" he whispered, and caught at his gun.

He was far too slow in his movements to match the skill and training of the sheriff. Now he stood at bay, his hand on the butt of the gun, his jaw set, his eyes wild, well covered by the gun of Wayland, as Barry Home stepped through the doorway.

"It's a plant, it's a plot!" muttered Rance Tucker, as he saw the face of Barry Home. "Home, he came here and put the stuff up there with the glass beads."

"You know too well where it came from," said the sheriff. "Cover this fellow a minute, Barry, while I go and call the others.

He stepped to the front door, and once more his voice rang into the night, more loudly than ever.

"Tom London! Oh, Tom! Come in! I've got him! Lew Tucker! Come in, Lew!"

Someone came, running.

"Be careful, and mind what you do," the voice of the sheriff said in caution. "Give me that gun, Lew. Now go ahead in and see the man we want. Why doesn't Tom come, too!"

The door of the kitchen flew open at the same moment that Lew Tucker stepped in from the hall, and there they saw Rance Tucker standing, covered by the supposed thief, and the sheriff assisting at this outrage.

But the very fact of that assistance struck the pair cold.

"There's the thief," said the sheriff, melodramatically, but most unnecessarily, as it seemed.

Mrs. Tucker had been drying her hands on her apron. She began to moan, saying: "Oh, Rance, I always knowed that God wouldn't let it be, with such an honest young fellow as Barry Home. You should've picked on that worthless Slim Farrar."

"I'm gonna say one thing," said Tucker, at last. "You've got me, but get the man that done the real job. Get Tom London. He robbed the coach!"

CHAPTER 16
The Pursuit

BUT NO MATTER HOW LOUDLY THE VOICE OF THE SHERiff had rung through the night, Tom London had not appeared. "He's gone!" said Barry Home, suddenly, and pointed toward the window.

What meant something to him, and very little to the others, was the small round eye of darkness, through which the bullets of Rance Tucker had sped not so long before.

A man could have seen a very informing tableau by looking through that peephole, at any time in the last minute or so, and what would keep Tom London from taking such a glance as he came running to answer the call of the sheriff?

"He's gone!" repeated Barry Home. "But he can't go as fast as I'll follow. Wayland, swear me in, make me deputy for this one night. Swear me, and I'll chase him to the rim of hell!"

Never was an oath administered more swiftly than at that particular moment.

And with the response trailing in the air behind him, Barry Home bolted from the house. As he ran from the door into the terrible blast of the wind, he saw what he expected, the silhouette of a horseman galloping up the road toward Loomis, with the gale helping him on. And the horse that he rode was a thoroughbred!

Groaning, staggering with a blindness of rage, and of helplessness, Barry Home rushed to where the long, low-built blue roan had been left.

Soon he was out on the road and there was the shadowy form of the fugitive not so far ahead, strangely close, as though he had halted to make some adjustment of his saddle and then had gone on.

But the blue roan was flying at full speed.

The wind had shifted a few points; the sky was scoured clean of clouds; and the moon poured a steady flood of silver into the pass as Barry Home rushed his horse up the trail. Well shod was the roan and sure-footed as a mustang has to be in the West, and he strode mightily on, the wind giving him wings.

Now Home could tell why, to his unutterable amazement he gained ground. As he drew closer, he could see the long-legged thoroughbred slipping and sliding in the treacherous going.

The surface of the road had been whipped clean of all snow by the force of the wind, but the earliest fall, that had melted, had turned to ice, and it was over a surface of ice that the cleated shoes of the gelding were beating, biting in to get a good grip and sending him swiftly and safely along.

Ah, trust Patty Loomis to have a horse that was a horse! And a rage of self-confidence swelled up in Barry and mastered him. He rode well forward, jockeying the good mustang, holding it with an iron hand, one hand, and that the left, because the right hand had to be nourished in the warmth of his body against the moment when it would be needed to grasp the handle of the Colt.

He could see, before him, how Tom London was riding his horse all out, now glancing back over his shoulder, now flogging the poor skidding thoroughbred to more frantic efforts.

Given one good mile of clear going, and there would be no doubt of how that exquisite mechanism of flesh and blood would speed away from the blue roan, but now the thoroughbred was caught at exactly the wrong moment and the low-running mustang made every stride a winning one. Tom London knew it, finally. He pulled up the horse at the side of the road, swung down to the ground, and drew his revolver.

It was still a good distance, fifty or sixty yards. There were two ways to manage the thing, to pull up the mustang in turn, and shoot it out at long range, or else to charge straight in, trusting that the motion of his gelding would upset the aim of London as much as it unsteadied his own hand.

The second course was the only one for Barry Home. As he snatched out his revolver, it seemed to him that he was merely an instrument in the hands of a greater fate which would control this battle.

There was no doubt in him. Calmly and coldly, but with the whole long agony of three discredited years weighing down upon him, he watched the gun of Tom London, as the robber fired. And he saw the moon flash dimly on the buttons of the man's heavy overcoat.

Then he fired in turn.

There seemed to be no effect. It was merely that Tom London had lowered his own weapon and seemed to be looking curiously at the charge of his enemy.

Then his knees sagged and he leaned over, very slowly, put out a hand toward the road and then collapsed.

He was dead. The certainty of it was in Barry

Home before he could rein up the gelding, and then turn back to the place.

Tom London was dead, and his horse was backing away from the horrible smell of blood.

They had sat long over the table at the Loomis hotel, because there was much to discuss out of that day's happenings, and the sudden disappearance of London, Rance Tucker and Barry Home, to say nothing of the sheriff, was enough to cause every man to hazard some conjecture.

There was the pale, drawn face of Patty Loomis, too, to cause the whispers to be lowered still further, as she circulated about the long dining table, laden with plates or platters. There was, too, the sombre look of Dave Loomis, sitting miserably at the head of the table robbed of his customary cheerfulness.

But three miles, even through bad weather, does not take a galloping horse much time. And they were still sitting about the table at the Loomis hotel when the door opened, and the sheriff looked in.

"I want to swear in a coupla deputies," he said, briefly.

Patty Loomis, with a moan, put her hand against the wall to steady herself.

The sheriff said to her, briskly: "It's not to get Barry Home, Patty. Barry Home needs no getting. There never was a time when he ought to've been got. Tom London robbed the Crystal Creek stage, and Barry's killed him for it—killed him resisting arrest, as an officer of the law. Rance Tucker went halves with London for putting the blame on poor Barry Home. And it's Rance that I want watched tonight. Any volunteers? Patty, I think Barry went around the back of the hotel."

She found him in the kitchen, sitting with his head resting in his hands.

After she had looked at him a moment, smiling

sadly and happily as well, she went to him and laid a hand on his shoulders.

"I know, Patty," said he. "I'll be all right in a minute. But I'm still a little sick. I've thought all the time that it was my business, only. Now I see that Fate or something had a hand in it all the while. Patty, I've killed a man!"

She was perfectly silent. Her face was grave. And she looked above and beyond him, as one who knows that happiness is near, but that it must be fought for to be kept.

BLACK THUNDER

CHAPTER 1

THE STONE WAS QUARTZITE AND THE DRILL WAS DULL—
yet Harrigan sank the hole rapidly, swinging the
twelve-pound hammer in a sort of fury. The hill-
side was a burning furnace of noonday heat—yet
Harrigan would not abate his labor.

The sweat blackened the back of his flannel shirt
in an irregular pattern that was watermarked
with salt at the edges. That back rose and fell a
little with every stroke. The shoulders worked.
Two mighty, elastic ropes of muscle sprang up
from the waist and spread powerful fingers across
the shoulder blades. But in spite of the strength
of this man, one could not help expecting him to
weaken and seek rest.

Yet he did not rest. He continued steadily at his
labor. An inexhaustible fuel, in fact, was being fed
into the furnace of this man's strength, and the
fuel was anger!

It was not merely the heat of the sun or of his
labor that kept the face of Dan Harrigan red. It
was not the effort of his labor that made his blue

eyes gleam. It was a steady passion of anger that set his jaws and lighted his eyes from a fire of the soul. Rage was to him like a sustaining food.

A mule brayed in the valley, and Harrigan leaped to his feet. He looked down toward the water hole in high hopes. But those hopes vanished. It was not MacTee, returning at last from town. Their mule was a piebald brute, and this was the usual dust-covered beast of burden, with a man on its back. The rider, plainly not MacTee, had just left the water hole, and was heading his mount up the half-mile grade toward the mine.

Harrigan pondered this. For twenty-four hours, MacTee had been due back from town, with supplies. Yet he had not come! What, then, had happened? Had he fallen into a brawl in the town? Had the dark passions of his Scotch nature boiled up until a forty-five caliber bullet quieted them forever? Had that great soul, that stark and terrible spirit vanished from the earth?

Harrigan was stunned by the mere suspicion that such a thing might be. He looked up at the sky, which was pale with the flood of the sunlight, and told himself that if MacTee had died, those heavens would be overcast by thunderheads. There would have been a sign of some sort even in the middle of the night. Lightning and sounds of doom would have accompanied the passing of MacTee.

And yet what could this be but a messenger to tell him of MacTee? What else would bring a man into the white heat of this desert? Not even buzzards wheeled in the air above the waste. Only the partnership of a MacTee and a Harrigan could have produced enough vital energy to drive men out here prospecting for gold. For two months they had broken ground, hoping that a thin vein of ore would widen. It had been bitterly hard, but

Harrigan and MacTee were used to bitter hardships. They were, in fact, used to one another!

The mule came nodding up the slope. The rider had bent his head. His hands were folded on the pommel of the saddle. He would be terribly thirsty. Harrigan turned with a sigh and contemplated the jug wrapped in sacking which was placed in a shadowy nook where the wind would strike it.

The man came nearer. The bristles on his unshaven face glinted in the sun. He was as big as MacTee, Harrigan decided. He carried a rifle in a long saddle-holster. There was a gun belt strapped about his hips. A big canteen bumped against the front of the saddle.

That was good. At least, he carried his own water with him!

Now he pulled up the mule close by the mine and dismounted. He looked young in years but old in the West. He stood still for a moment, staring at Harrigan, and the waves of heat rose with a dull shimmering from his sombrero. He was as lean as a desert wolf, all skin and bones and sheer power.

"Howdy," he said. "This is about the middle of hell, ain't it?"

"Yeah," said Harrigan. "This is the corner of Main Street and First Avenue, in the center of Hell. You couldn't be wrong."

"All right," said the stranger. "Then you're Harrigan."

"Yes. I'm Harrigan."

"If you're Harrigan, where's MacTee?"

"He's not here," said Harrigan.

"You lie," said the man of the guns.

Suddenly Harrigan straightened. He seemed to grow younger. A tender light came into his eyes.

"Brother," said he, in the softest of voices, "did you call me a liar?"

"I asked for MacTee, and you say that he ain't here!" protested the other. "If he ain't here, where is he?"

"He's in Dunphyville, yonder."

"You lie again," said the stranger. "There ain't hardly enough left of Dunphyville to cover a prairie dog. If a jackrabbit tried to hide behind what's left of Dunphyville, his ears would stick up behind the heap."

"That's twice in a row that I've been a liar," counted Harrigan, rubbing his hands together and looking rather wistfully into the face of the newcomer. "What's your name?"

"Rollo Quay," said the big man.

"Rollo," said Harrigan, "it's a funny name. It ain't the only funny thing about you, neither. But before I make you any funnier, I want to find out what happened to Dunphyville."

"It was wrecked," said Quay.

"I don't know how God, man, or the devil could want to waste time to wreck that dump," said Harrigan.

"It wasn't a God, man, or devil that wrecked the place. It was MacTee," said Quay.

Harrigan nodded.

"MacTee got restless, did he?" said Harrigan. "Well, if he got careless and stubbed his toe on a place like Dunphyville, I guess there's not much left of the town."

"There ain't gonna be much left of MacTee, when I find him," said Quay. "Not when I meet him, there ain't gonna be!—I'm gunna take payment out of his black hide for everything he did to my saloon back there in Dunphyville!"

"Brother," said Harrigan, "I hear you talk, and I'd certainly like to save you till you had a chance to meet him. But I don't think that I can wait that long. What was the last seen of MacTee in Dunphyville?"

"The last seen of him," said Quay, "was a cloud of dust with a streak of lightnin' through it. Nobody knows exactly where it landed. And nobody knows exactly where it disappeared to. But before I talk about Black MacTee anymore, I'm gonna do something to make Red Harrigan a little bit redder. You Irish son of a hoop-snake and a bobtailed lynx, I'm gunna take you apart, first, and find out where that skunk of a MacTee is, later on."

He stepped straight forward, feinted in workmanlike manner with his left, and drove an excellent right for the head.

Harrigan ducked his head half an inch and shed that punch as a rock sheds waters.

"Here's the same sock with a hook to it," said Harrigan, and knocked Mr. Quay under the feet of the mule.

Rollo Quay sat up half a minute later and laid one hand on the side of his jaw. Then he saw that Harrigan was sitting on the back of the mule. The revolvers that Quay reached for were gone.

"I'll leave the mule in Dunphyville, safe and sound," said Harrigan.

"Damn the mule," said Quay. "What I want to know is—where did you hide that blackjack when your sleeves was turned up to the elbow."

"That was no blackjack. That was the hook in the end of that punch," said Harrigan. "I'm going to look for MacTee. If he happens to drop in here while I'm gone, talk soft and low to him, brother. I'm only a sort of chore boy around here. But Black MacTee is a *man*!"

CHAPTER 2
Where the Lightning Struck

THERE WERE ONLY A DOZEN BUILDINGS IN DUNPHY-
ville, but they all seemed in place to the eye of
Harrigan, as he drew near the town. In spite of
the storm of which Quay had spoken, nothing appeared wrong, until Harrigan entered the single
street.

Then he noted sundry details of interest. Most
of the windows were broken. The chairs on the
front verandah of the hotel were missing one leg
or two, and several of them had been converted
into stools. All the "e's" in the sign "General Merchandise Store" had disappeared and were rep-
resented by ragged eyeholes of light. And the
whole side of the blacksmith shop was scorched
and the ground blackened beside it, as though the
dead grass had been kindled in an effort to burn
the town.

Harrigan stopped the mule in front of the saloon. The two swinging doors were gone. The two
front windows were smashed out. Broken glass
glittered in the dust of the street. One of the frail

114

wooden pillars that held up the roof over the verandah was broken in the middle and sagged to the side. The darkness inside had about it an empty air of desolation.

"Yes," murmured Harrigan, "it looks like Black MacTee!"

He dismounted from the mule, made comfortable the revolver which was under his coat, and entered the saloon through the open doorway.

It was indeed an empty spot.

Of the long mirror that had reflected so many sunburned faces there remained against the wall only a few shreds of brightness and gilding. Of the long array of bottles whose necks and brilliant labels had shone on the shelf behind the bar, all were gone except half a dozen lonely last survivors. The brass rail was bent and broken from its brackets. Bullets had ripped the polished surface of the bar itself. And behind the bar leaned the one-time stalwart figure of a fat man in a dirty apron. He wore a plaster over one cheek, a leather patch over one eye, a red-stained bandage around his head, and his left arm was supported in a sling.

"Hello," said Harrigan. "What happened?"

The barman looked toward Harrigan with one dull eye.

"Hullo," he said, in a hollow voice. "There was a kind of an explosion. After that, I don't seem to remember nothin' very clear."

"Let's have a drink," said Harrigan, putting one elbow on the splintered edge of the bar.

"There ain't nothing to drink except brandy at a dollar a throw," said the barman, "All the rest—"

He made a vague gesture with one hand. He turned to follow his own gesture and survey the destruction.

"We'll have the brandy, then," said Harrigan.

The barman found one of the few bottles that remained and set it with a glass before Harrigan.

"You're drinking, too," said Harrigan.

The barman filled a glass for himself, sadly.

"Now," said Harrigan. "What happened the other day when Black MacTee was here?"

"It all started right over there in the corner," said the barman. "MacTee was loaded up to start for his mine. His mule was hitched outside the door. And MacTee was settin' there in the corner, readin' a stack of the old newspapers that we keep there. There was a dozen of the boys in here, most of them from the Curley Ranch."

He paused, refilled his brandy glass by sense of touch while his eyes still contemplated the memory.

"All I recollect after that," said the barman, "ain't very much. I remember that MacTee come over here to the bar and set 'em up all around for the boys. They all drank, and he set 'em up again. And then he lifted up his whisky glass and he hollered out: 'To Kate, boys—' "

"My God!" said Harrigan. "What was it he said? 'To Kate?' What put him on that track? What newspaper was he reading? Tell me, man—what newspaper was he reading?"

The flame of his hair was the flame of his eyes. He devoured the very soul of the man before him.

"Wait a minute. Don't hurry me or I'm gonna have a relapse," said the bartender. "He ups with his glass and says: 'To Kate.' And everybody hollers out and downs the drink, except me. And when he sees that my glass is still full, he says what's the matter with me, and I say no disrespect to the Kate that he knows, but that once I got tangled up with a freckle-faced snake by that name, and ever since, when I heard the name of Kate, I got shootin' pains and colic. Well, I no sooner says that, than he reaches across the bar and slams me, and I drop off into a deep sleep. When I wake up, this here is what I see!"

"Kate!" said Harrigan. "He's spotted her! He's gone! For the love of the dear God, tell me, man, where's the newspaper that he was reading when he let out that Indian yell?"

"Where's the beer gone, and the soda, and the bar whiskey and—"

"Shut up!" said Harrigan. And the barman was silent, for he found in the eye of Harrigan something that was hard to meet. The blank fury of the great MacTee was not as terrible as the blue lightning that was now in the eyes of Harrigan.

"How far to the railroad?" demanded Harrigan.

"Seven miles," gasped the barman.

"Tell Quay, when he comes back, that his mule will be over at the railroad. So long!"

And Harrigan fled through the doorway and leaped into the saddle on the mule's back.

CHAPTER 3
On the Trail of Black MacTee

THE TOWN OF CALDWELL JUNCTION CONTAINED NOT A great many more buildings than Dunphyville, outside of the railroad station and the sheds. In such a small town it was not surprising, therefore, that the first thing Harrigan saw was the pinto mule with the black and white tail, standing outside of the grocery store. The grocer himself was loading a wicker basket, filled with supplies, into a cart to which the mule was hitched.

"Where'd you get the mule?" asked Harrigan.

The grocer was pink and white. All grocers have that complexion. His pink turned to red, and his white turned to pink, when he faced Harrigan.

"There was a man here the other day—" he said.

"Big—black hair—drunk—happy?" asked Harrigan.

"Yes," said the grocer. "What has he done? Are you after him? Who is he?"

"He's a double-crossing Scotch black-souled hound," said Harrigan. "Did you buy this mule from him?"

"Yes," said the grocer, shrinking from the red and blue flame of Harrigan.

Harrigan groaned, in his mind's eye was the haunting picture of a lovely girl whose given name was Kate.

"The big man with the black eyes, he pulled out of this town on a train, I don't doubt. What train was it?"

"It was headed south. It was a freight," said the grocer, rather frightened.

"What train is this one?" asked Harrigan suddenly, as a whistle shrieked up the track.

"That's the Overland, bound south," said the grocer.

"Then it doesn't stop here?"

"No. It just takes the grade slow, and—"

But Harrigan, without waiting to hear more, without waiting for the money that had been promised, turned and sprinted down the street. He saw the engine's head come nobly into view, swaying with speed. He saw that speed quenched somewhat by the upgrade passing the Junction. But still the train was thundering along, dust and cinders whipping under its wheels as it shot by the station.

Harrigan, turning with it as the tender went by, sprinted with all his might. He reached his full speed as the observation car went past and he leaped high and far for the iron balustrade that fenced in the rear platform.

He caught with both hands. The grip of one was broken. For an instant his body streamed out behind the flying train. Then he drew himself lightly up and scrambled aboard.

The conductor came on the run, half a minute later. He took Harrigan by the collar.

"Bums like you *oughta* die!" said the conductor. "I've a mind to throw you off now. If we weren't behind time, I'd stop the train on the trestle, and heave you off into the gulch. But when we hit the next stop you'll be on your way to jail, young fellow!"

Said Harrigan: "You're mistaking me, my friend. My brother-in-law, Mr. Peter Van Houston Dyce, is on board this train. I had to ride fifty miles to get here to tell him that his father has just been roughed by a bear on my ranch."

"Get out of this observation car and stand on the front platform, you lying bum!" said the conductor.

So Harrigan stood for eighty miles on the front platform, and smiled as he heard the roar of the wheels and their rapid syncopation over the tracks.

It was nearing dusk when they reached the next stop. Harrigan slid off on the blind side of the train, and walked ahead as far as the first signal light. When the train passed that point, gathering speed, it gathered Harrigan, also, into its blind baggage.

The vigilance of the conductor, who was led by a spirit of eerie inquiry, found Harrigan on the blind baggage, fifty miles farther south. He tried to brain Harrigan with a signal lantern, but the redheaded man escaped. He rode another seventy miles on the tops of the coaches, or between them, but at the last he was driven from this refuge.

The whole train crew, by this time, had sharpened its eyes, hardened its fists, and roused its soul for this contest with a daring tramp. But it was not until the gray of the dawn that Harrigan, after haunting that express all through the night, at last, left the Overland. He would not have left it even then, except that he began to feel that perhaps he had overstepped his proper distance south. Therefore, in fear that Black MacTee might have ceased travelling in this direction, he dropped off at the railroad yards of a big cattle-shipping town to look about him and make inquiry.

Three railroad detectives closed suddenly on him like three little kingbirds on one big hawk. He did not run. He did not fight. He let two of them hold him by the arms while the third rammed the muzzle of a revolver into the pit of his stomach.

"You're Harrigan," said the third man.

"With that gun in front of you, you can call me worse things than that," said Harrigan.

"It's a big rap that you've got to stand for," said the detective.

"What's the charge against me?" asked Harrigan, "and who made it?"

"You murdered Joe Chantry, up yonder," said the man who carried the gun. "And the gent that told us about you is the man that you're chasing south. He's the next one that you want to bump off. He didn't look like the sort of a bird who'd run away, neither."

Harrigan blinked.

"As big as me, or bigger?" he asked. "Black hair and black eyes and a dark skin?"

"Yes," said the man with the gun. "Come along, Harrigan. He warned us that you're likely to make trouble. But the first trouble you start with us is gunna break your back and split your wishbone. Understand?"

"I understand," said Harrigan, "that he'd have me hanged to get me off his trail, and be damned to him! It's Black MacTee, and gone blacker than ever! Oh, yes, I understand. I never heard of a man called Joe Chantry—but I understand!"

He was marching forward with a man on either arm, and the man with the gun behind him. Now he stumbled, or seemed to stumble, and kicked out behind him with the fine precision of an army mule. The gun carrier shot a hole in the morning sky and went down with a pair of battered shins. Harrigan threw the other two detectives on top of him, collected three guns, and ran toward the rumbling sound of a long freight that was pulling out on the southern route.

It was a train of empties. He hooked his ride, found a boxcar, and slipped through the open door. On the floor he sat while the dust danced on the trembling boards and the landscape swept by him. Mountains near and far, then a series of black tunnels, with open country beyond, a smiling land of rolling hills with groves of trees shading it, and the flash of water running in every valley.

They passed the scattered houses of another large cow-town. As the train slowed, Harrigan left the three revolvers in the boxcar and swung down to the ground. He had to sprint hard, because the train was still travelling fast. And while he was still helpless with the speed of his running, trying to keep from pitching forward on his face, leaning back his head and shoulders, he saw a long, lean man with a deep-visored cap pulled well over his eyes, come out from behind one of the piles of ties that were corded here at the end of the railroad yard.

This man raised a hand with the bright flash of a gun in it. Harrigan had been running as fast as he could, before this. He tried now to increase his speed. The end of the freight train went by with a departing thunder. He heard the voice of the man with the gun shouting for him to stop. A gun barked. But Harrigan dived the next instant around the corner of one of the big stacks of ties.

There he waited. He looked down at his shoulder and saw the glint of bare skin. The bullet had nipped away a bit of the strong flannel cloth.

Footfalls rushed up, crunching on the cinders. A shadow sloped over the ground around the corner of the ties. So Harrigan sprang at that instant and laid the barrel of his gun along the head of the pursuer.

Afterward he sat the limp body on the ground and waited for life to return to the eyes. He picked up the fallen revolver. Inside the coat of the man he found the shield of a railroad detective. Up the sleeve of the coat, he found a handy blackjack.

His victim groaned. Harrigan took the man by his long chin and shook his head violently.

"Brother," said Harrigan, looking down into the bright, dangerous eyes, "you're another that MacTee has made a fool of. He's told you to look out for Harrigan. He's told you that Harrigan is wanted for the killing of a fellow named Chantry. Well, boy, I never heard of a gent named Chantry and that's a fact! But I've heard of Black MacTee. Where is he? Which way did he go? Further south?"

The bright little eyes looked at Harrigan without expression. They were simply bright.

"All right," said Harrigan. "I hate to do it, but I'm fighting against time."

He took the hand of the detective, pulled his arm rigid, and then tapped him with the blackjack across the ridge of the tight shoulder muscles.

The detective closed his eyes and turned gray-green. Harrigan took the other arm, jerked it tight, brought down the blackjack on a similar spot.

"All right," said the detective. "That's enough." His eyes opened again. "Why not?" he said. "I don't know what the game is that you two thugs are playing, but I know that I *want* you to meet. He left the railroad line, right here. I dunno where he faded to."

Harrigan went to a barbershop for a shave. The barber was so fat that even the effort of standing made him pant a little.

"I read something in the paper, a while ago," Harrigan remarked, deciding to try a shot in the dark. "The news came from here. It was about a girl with an Irish name. Her name is Kate Malone—"

"She ain't from here," said the barber. "You mean the schoolteacher that saved her pupils when the school caught on fire?"

"That's the one," said Harrigan.

"She ain't from here," said the barber. "She's teaching a crossroads school eight miles out on the Cullen Road."

Harrigan left the shop and went to a clothing store. He bought a necktie and a cheap coat, then found the Cullen Road. A buckboard drew up from behind, stopped, took him in without a word. The driver was a grim-faced rancher who kept looking straight before him and never spoke.

"I'm trying to locate my sister, Kate Malone," said Harrigan.

The rancher turned his head a little, but looked at the distance, instead of at Harrigan.

"I reckon that she's found a whole crop of brothers, since the school burned down," said he.

He spoke no more for an hour. The green hills drifted slowly behind them while the two mustangs dogtrotted sullenly along, heads down, enduring the miles.

At last, the old rancher pulled up the team and pointed to a cluster of trees around a red roof.

"That's the Tyndale house," he said. "That's where Kate Malone is living while the school's rebuilding. I hope she remembers your face, young man!"

CHAPTER 4
Black MacTee

THERE WAS A PLEASANT WIND THAT TUMBLED A FEW white clouds across the sky. The hills were the finest Harrigan ever had seen. Never had there been such cattle as those which dotted the wide range. The very air was different, for Kate Malone also was breathing it!

He went up the side lane, opened the gate and passed on to the house. A negro in a cook's apron was carrying stove wood from the woodshed toward the kitchen door. Down the slope behind the house Harrigan saw, through the tree trunks, the gleam of running water.

"I'm looking for Angus MacTee," said Harrigan.

"Yes, sir," said the cook. "I guess he ain't here, sir."

"No?" said Harrigan. "Is Miss Kate Malone here then?"

"No, sir, I guess she ain't here, neither." The cook rolled his eyes. "She was called away sir," he said, "by a message from town, and—"

Harrigan grinned, suddenly.

"How much did MacTee pay you for telling me that lie?" he asked. "Ten dollars?"

"No, sir. Five dollars," said the cook. "I mean—"

He stopped short, his thick lips parted, his eyes perfectly rounded as he saw that he had been so easily trapped.

"Is MacTee here now?" asked Harrigan.

"He—he—" stammered the cook. "I guess so."

"Is he down there by the creek? Is he with her?" asked Harrigan, pointing.

The cook was silent, agape. So Harrigan marched straight down the hill, through the heat of the sun and the cool touch of the shadows, until he came close to the edge of the water. Then he heard voices, and slipped from tree to tree until he could see Kate Malone herself sitting on a rock at the side of the stream. The current curved toward the other bank, at this point, and in the still eddy lay the image of the girl with a patch of sun in her hair. Black Angus MacTee stood beside her.

Since she was turned away from him, somewhat, MacTee did not need to guard his facial expression. Under the great dark ridges of his brows, his eyes burned with a black fire.

When Harrigan saw the man, it seemed to him that he was dwarfed by the dimensions of MacTee and by the pride and furious, headlong desire in the face of the man.

"What I want to know is not much, Kate," said Angus MacTee. "It's only to find out if you mind me being here close to you. It's only to find out if you care the least mite for me, Kate."

She looked up, not at MacTee, but at the long, bright slope of the hill beyond the creek.

"I've owed my life to you, Angus," said the girl. "How could I help caring for you? Except for you and Dan Harrigan—"

"Poor Harrigan," said MacTee. "*There* was a man!"

The girl got up from her place and looked straight into the face of MacTee. And Harrigan would have given worlds to have been standing nearer to study her expression.

"Is Dan Harrigan dead?" she asked. Her voice was level. Who could tell what emotion was behind it?

"If he were dead, would it be breaking your heart, Kate?" asked MacTee.

"He's not dead, Angus," said the girl. "I know the two of you. I know that better friends never lived in the world than you are. If Danny were dead, you couldn't speak of him with a still eye, Angus."

"I was his friend," agreed Angus MacTee, with a ponderous sigh. "But now I'm thinking that it might be better for Dan if he were under the ground."

He turned away, slightly, from the girl. And Harrigan closed his hands to fists.

"What's happened to him?" asked Kate Malone.

"Whisky got him," answered MacTee. "Whisky got poor Dan. It was so that I didn't care to let him go to town alone. He'd spend the money I gave him for groceries, on nothing but whisky. I'd have to go in afterwards, and I'd find him with his money spent, singing in a saloon for more drinks, or holding out his hand on a street corner—"

Harrigan leaned his forehead against the trunk of a tree and fought back the growl that was rising in his throat.

"Poor Danny!" cried the girl. "I know how it is with great big impulsive natures like his! Oh, poor Danny."

Life returned to Harrigan, as he listened.

"If that was only the worst!" sighed MacTee. "But it's not the worst. Whisky takes hold of a man, Kate, and rots the heart in him. Whisky turns the soul in a man. Poor Harrigan! I'm afraid he's done for now. The law's after him, Kate."

"For what?" she cried.

"Don't talk of it, Kate," muttered MacTee. "Don't have words about it. I wouldn't breathe it even to you. Murder's not a thing to be talked about, is it?"

"Murder!" she gasped. Then: "I've got to go to him, Angus. He needs me, and I've got to go to him!"

"Eh?" grunted MacTee, staggered by this result of his talk.

"I've always sworn that if either of you were in trouble, I'd go around the world to help you. And he needs me now."

"You'd do him good if he were like his old self," said MacTee, shaking his head. "But there's little left of the old Dan Harrigan. Ah, when I think of the eye of him, and the fire in his hair, and the fire in his heart, Kate, it's a pitiful thing to think of the man he is now, with his hair turning gray, and his eye dim, and his face all bloated. He looks old, Kate, and weak. The soul's gone out of him. He wouldn't want to lay eyes on you, Kate. It would remind him of the days when he was a man, and when he loved Kate Malone—if he really loved you, Kate! But I've always thought it was just that he saw I wanted you, and so he wanted you too. Except for him, tell me the truth of it, Kate—you and I would have been married long ago. You never would have run away from me, except for Dan Harrigan!"

"I won't talk of it, Angus," said the girl. "If Danny were here, I might try. But not when he's away."

"It's Harrigan that you loved, then?" exclaimed MacTee, with a terrible scowl. "When you ran away and left word behind you, you said in the letter that you really loved one of us, but you wouldn't choose him for fear the other of us would be murdering the lucky one."

"You know well how it was," answered Kate Malone. "I owed my life to you, both. You were greater friends than I've ever seen in the world. But if I married one of you, the other one would be unhappy. And men like you and Dan, Angus, are sure to use your hands, when you're unhappy. That was why I ran away. But if Danny is ill, I've got to find him. You must take me to him, Angus!"

"He won't need to take you, Kate," said the great Harrigan, and stepped out from his shelter.

She put out her hands toward him. He saw the terror of inquiry turn to joy in her eyes. She ran to him and he leaned over her and kissed her.

"Angus, Angus!" said the girl. "How could you have played such a joke on me, with Danny standing there all the time?"

MacTee was black indeed. His great hands hooked themselves into predacious claws. His body trembled with passion. But he strove to cover this emotion with a harsh, grinding laugh.

"I wanted to surprise you, Kate," said MacTee. "And then have old Danny jump out like a Jack-in-the-box. Good old Danny!"

Cheerfully he smote the shoulder of Harrigan, a blow that would have felled an ordinary man.

"Damn your black heart, you sneaking traitor," murmured Harrigan, adding aloud: "Well, well— old Angus! He carried it pretty far, though. 'Bloated face'—eh? There's the bright young wit for you! There's the boy to make the crowd laugh! Kate, let me look at you. Let me soak you up with my eyes. God bless me, it's a happy day, even if there's a Black MacTee in it!"

Her blue eyes were shining into the blue eyes of Harrigan. But the joy bubbling up in her grew suddenly dim, when she heard Harrigan end on the remark about MacTee.

"I wouldn't want to spoil any party," said MacTee, coldly. "I'll step along, Kate. You and Dan seem to have a lot to say to each other."

"Stop it, Angus!" she exclaimed. "Stop it, Dan. You're glaring at one another like two wolves. Can't we be three friends together? Can't we—"

She stopped, with a groan of despair.

"Sure," said Harrigan. "We're all friends together."

But still his eyes were fastened on those of MacTee, blue fire on black fire.

And the girl, glancing from one to the other, turned pale. The happiness was gone from her as suddenly as it had come.

But she made herself say, cheerfully: "We'll take a walk together, and talk over everything since we were last together. I'll just run up to the house for ten minutes to change these shoes, and then we'll take a stroll over the hills. Wait here!"

She hurried up among the trees toward the house, turning once to wave and smile toward them, before disappearing.

CHAPTER 5
Brothers of Battle

WHEN THEY WERE ALONE, EACH OF THEM TOOK A LONG stride that left them closely confronting one another.

"Only one of us is going to be here when she comes back," said the Black MacTee.

"Ay," answered Harrigan. "Only one of us. You murdering thug, I'm going to take everything out of you. You ran off with the mule. You left me to starve at the mine. You chucked away our money. You planted the railroad dicks along the trail to salt me down with lead if they had a chance. But all that's nothing. You had to lie to Kate Malone about me. You had to tell her that I'm a worthless drunk. Damn you, I'm going to take all of that out of you."

"I told her the truth about what you're going to be, Harrigan," said MacTee. "Because when I get through with you, today, you're going to be afraid to lift your head and look even a Chinaman in the face. I'm going to grind you so damn small, Harrigan, that the wind can blow you away."

"Perhaps," said Harrigan, "but not just now."

"You're turning yellow already, are you?" demanded MacTee. "You're trying to back down, are you? You're a rat!"

"MacTee," said Harrigan, "all the soul of me is itching in my hands. But we can't fight it out now. She'll be back before we could finish. Only, I promise you that you'll have your chance before the day's ended! We're going to take a walk, now, with Kate. We're going to be polite to each other. And tomorrow, one of us will either be dead or gone away. Is that right?"

MacTee, after fixing a glance of terrible disdain on Harrigan for a moment, turned on his heel and strode off to a small distance. He began to walk up and down, wrapped in his dark thoughts.

But Harrigan leaned against a tree and smoked a cigarette, and watched Angus MacTee. Dimly there passed through his mind the many pictures of the days when he had walked at the side of Angus MacTee into the face of dangers which they had met together. They had wrought such deeds for one another that the whole wide West had spoken of them. They had been such friends as men conceive, but never find.

Of these things, however, Harrigan saw only the faint pictures. For now they wanted one woman. In the old days they had done battle for her. Matched in strength, in craft, in desperate courage, Red Dan Harrigan and Black MacTee had struggled to win her, until in the end she had fled from them both for fear that they would kill one another. She had told them that they would never see her again. She had told them, in her last letter, that she truly loved one of them. But her choice she would not name.

When she was gone, they were to each other more than brothers. But now that she was with them again, they mutually poisoned the air for one another.

All this was in the mind of Harrigan, as he stared at MacTee. When they were together at the mine, the vigilance of MacTee in acts of courtesy and in kindness never ended. He was always first to find the water jar empty and to assume the labor of filling it. He was the first to forage for wood. He labored willingly extra hours sharpening the drills. The money in his pocket was Harrigan's money; the blood in his body was Harrigan's blood; the breath of his nostrils he would give up for his friend. But not Kate Malone!

When she entered their world, MacTee became a dark and crafty savage. A wild Indian was capable of no more atrocities. His fruitful malevolence had scattered a hundred dangers along the trail which Harrigan had just followed. It would scatter more, in the future. So there arose in Harrigan a red flame of detestation and hatred. If Kate Malone were removed, he knew that he and MacTee were welded as one flesh and one blood and one bone. That was the very reason she had fled from them before—

Suddenly Harrigan said: "MacTee, it's more than ten minutes we've been waiting."

"Ah?" muttered MacTee.

"It's nearer to fifteen," said Harrigan.

"What would you mean by that, and glaring at me?" asked MacTee.

"I'd mean," said Harrigan, "that you let the brute beast come out in your face, a minute ago, and she could see it plain enough. She's gone again—I'll bet my soul on it. She's gone again!"

MacTee gave him one stern glance.

"Maybe you're right. But it's the red hell that shone out of you, that she saw!"

They were already dashing through the woods toward the house.

"I might have guessed—" groaned Harrigan.

He strained with all his might to gain the lead. It seemed to him that in this contest the supremacy between them would be established. But when they issued from the trees before the house, MacTee was a stride in the lead.

Instantly they saw the answer to their fears. On a distant hill a rider wavered for an instant on the horizon, then disappeared from their view. It was a woman. It must be Kate Malone.

"Damn you!" said Harrigan, and smote the dark granite of the jaw of MacTee.

Stone is hard, but iron is harder, and the fist of Harrigan was iron. MacTee was hurled to the ground, and Harrigan ran toward a big, brown gelding that was tethered in front of the ranchhouse.

"Hey, boss, you ain't runnin' off with that hoss, are you?" shouted the cook.

Harrigan answered, merely: "I'll send back the price in hard cash!"

He untethered the rope with flying fingers. He had his foot in the stirrup, when a thunderbolt struck him to the ground.

It was Angus MacTee.

And it was Angus MacTee who leaped into the saddle. Harrigan rose and laid his mighty clutch on the reins, reaching for the gun hand of MacTee at the same time, and locking his hold on the wrist.

Then a calm voice said behind them: "You two hoss-thieves, get away from that mustang!"

They looked toward the house and saw on the verandah a little man with a long rifle levelled firmly at his shoulder.

There is no arguing with a rifle held by such hands. One may gamble against a revolver, but not against a rifleman who kills his deer at six hundred yards.

So MacTee dismounted and stood at the side of Harrigan.

"I oughta hold you and jail you, maybe," said the rancher. "But all I'll do is to get you off my place. Move, the pair of you!"

He raised his voice to an angry yell, as he lost control of his temper.

"Get!" he cried.

MacTee and Harrigan "got."

They strode rapidly across the rolling ground until they found the trail of the horse which had carried the girl away from them. They came to the hilltop over which she had dropped from view. There they paused.

They glared at one another with gloomy detestation. On the jaw of MacTee there was a red lump. On the side of Harrigan's face was its mate.

"Harrigan," said MacTee. "I'm going to break you open like a crab and eat the heart out of you, before long."

"MacTee," said Harrigan, "there's nothing here but the sky and the grass to look at us. I'm better than you with a gun. I'll put it aside. I'll have you with my bare hands. There'll be more taste to the killing of you, that way."

"Harrigan," said MacTee, "it's a true thing that I'd love to be at you. But we've got a job on our hands that may use up the brains of both of us. Look yonder!"

He pointed toward the wide landscape, the green hills, and the ragged storm of mountains that rose toward the horizon.

"There's our job. Kate's no fool. She's as tough as whipcord, and she'll run like a fox till she thinks that she's dropped us off her trail. She's dropped us before. She'll drop us again, unless we put our heads together and all the strength that's in us. Let's be partners again till we've found her. And afterwards—God help you, Harrigan!"

Red Dan Harrigan grinned. He held out his hand.

"I'll be a brother to you, MacTee," he said, "till we've found her. And after that, MacTee, I'll work you into a red mud, with my hands!"

Their hands closed, joining with a mighty pressure.

CHAPTER 6
Yellow Gulch

THEY TRAVELLED THROUGH THE REST OF THAT DAY AS only Harrigan and MacTee could travel. If there was more speed in MacTee's long legs over the level, there was more agility in Harrigan when they came to rough country. In the evening, they came to a little ranchhouse on the southern side of a hill. In a big field near the house and barn, horses were grazing.

Said MacTee: "We've got to have horses, if we want to find Kate Malone."

"We've got to find horses," agreed Harrigan. "But you know this part of the world, MacTee. They'd rather hang a horse thief than a murderer, Angus."

"There was never a rope spun that could hang me," said Angus MacTee. "If there's no heart in you, Harrigan, turn back, now, and I'll go on alone."

"How could a Scotchman have the heart of a Harrigan?" asked the other. "I'll go wherever you'll go, MacTee, and do whatever you'll do, and then one step beyond."

"Go into that barn, then, and find saddles and bridles," said MacTee, calmly, "and ropes. When you've got 'em, I'll catch the horses. I'm not as good a thief as you are. There's not much cat in me. But I can handle a rope."

It might seem an unfair division of the labor for Harrigan to risk the danger of men, and MacTee to take only the task of catching up horses. But Red Harrigan was not one to split straws. He circled the hill on which the ranch buildings stood, came over the shoulder of it, and passed out of the twilight into the thick, muddy black of the interior of the barn. Suddenly out of the darkness he heard the overbearing powerful neigh of a stallion. A horse began to plunge and batter inside a box stall. Harrigan groaned, for the people in the ranchhouse were sure to hear this uproar and respond to it. He was not surprised when, far away, he heard a screen door slam with a tin-pan jingling.

He had found saddles and saddle blankets and bridles. And now hurried back with them toward the rear door. He was not yet at it when the other door opened.

Harrigan, leaping eagerly into the outer night, found that he was lighted by the brightening moonlight. A man shouted loudly: "Stop, thief!"

Harrigan kicked the door shut behind him and ran into the field, the corner where MacTee was already holding a pair of mustangs. He reached MacTee, who held the horses steady while Harrigan began the saddling in frantic haste.

The near door of the barn opened. Harrigan groaned. But he could hear the man who stood in the entrance swearing angrily, apparently unable to see anything suspicious.

The rancher fired twice, but the bullets came nowhere near the two thieves. Then he cried out, loudly, as other men came running from the house.

But Harrigan and MacTee were already spurring away. The instant they were seen, bullets came whirring. But what can a revolver do at long range when it is fired by moonlight? They rode straight on up a narrow valley, the floor of which grew steeper and steeper.

MacTee began to laugh.

"Dan, d'ye hear me? Isn't it like the old days? Were there ever any better days than the old ones?"

And Dan Harrigan laughed, too. He forgot Kate Malone. He forgot the very object of his quest. It seemed to him that there was nothing in the world that was half so important as the great Black MacTee, the companion who never failed a man in time of danger. Behind them came the noise of hoofs. But the two merely laughed again, in the highest indifference. Mere mortals could not be matched against a Harrigan and a Black MacTee.

For two hours, off and on, they heard the distant noise of the pursuit. Twice rifles were fired after them. Then they were left alone to travel deeper into the night.

"Suppose that she left this trail?" asked Harrigan.

"She'd keep to the valley," answered MacTee. "I know the way her mind works. She'd keep to this valley. She'd want to get those mountains for a fence between her and Harrigan and MacTee."

A wind struck them, iced by the high mountain snows. But they held steadily on, crossed the divide, and came down through tall forests. At last, staring through a gap in the woods, they made out the widespread, gleaming lights of a town.

"That's where she is," said MacTee, with great assurance. "There's no use killing the horses. We'll go down in the morning, and find her there."

"She'll start on before the morning," said Harrigan.

"She can't keep running all the way around the world," answered MacTee. "No, she'll stay there for a while and hope that we'll never find her. We'd better camp here."

So they camped. They built a bed of evergreen boughs and were soon asleep. And when they wakened, the sky was luminous with the dawn. They resaddled the horses, pulled up their belts a notch, and jogged the mustangs down toward the town.

It was sprawled like a spider, with a small body and with long arms that stretched up many narrow gulches round about. Twenty trails converged on that small city.

"It's a jumping-off place," said Harrigan, gloomily. "She might have gone in any direction!"

"We'll find her," said MacTee. "There's something in me that knows how to find her as sure as a magnet knows how to find north!"

The trail down was slow work. It was very rough and entailed constant windings that absorbed much time. The sun was high and hot when at last they dropped into the hollow where the town lay.

MacTee wanted to go straight to the hotel.

"Suppose a pair of stolen horses have been trailed as far as this town?" suggested Harrigan, uneasily.

"We have to take chances," answered MacTee. "And in the hotel, we'll find people who'll know every stray dog that's entered the town in the last ten years."

They reached the hotel, which was a square white box shouldered tightly in between adjoining buildings, with the usual verandah strung across the face of it. In a livery stable across the street they put up the horses, then entered the hotel. They washed and shaved, and went into the dining room.

It was after eight o'clock, and, therefore, very late for breakfast in a Western town. The chairs were standing on tables. A big fellow with a tattooed arm of a sailor was scrubbing the floor with a pail of suds and a stable broom.

"Too late, brother!" he growled over his shoulder at the pair.

MacTee took two chairs from a small table and put them in place.

"Ham and eggs, coffee, hotcakes, and anything else that's handy," said he.

The waiter walked up to him with a scowl.

"Are you tryin' to start something?" he demanded.

MacTee put the end of a forefinger against the breast of the ex-sailor. It was like touching him with a rod of steel.

"What I start, I finish," said MacTee. "Unless you want to be close to the end, move some chuck out of the kitchen and into this room. Understand?"

The waiter understood. He moved his glance in a small arc, from the third button of MacTee's shirt to his gleaming eyes.

"All right," said the waiter, and nodded.

MacTee and Harrigan sat down.

"Danny," said MacTee, "I wish that we'd never laid eyes on Kate Malone."

"I wish it, too," said Harrigan, "except when I think of her."

"She's nothing," said MacTee, "but a snip of a girl with a brown face and blue eyes. There's a thousand prettier than she is. What is she to come between friends like you and me?"

Harrigan frowned and shook his head.

"I'd like to agree with you, Angus," said he. "But I'm just after seeing her. Besides, you'd never hold to the idea that you have right now. Not if you thought that I had Kate Malone."

"No," agreed MacTee, suddenly. He jarred the heavy table with one fist. "You and I have fought for her and starved for her and bled for her too many times. I couldn't give her up to you, Danny. But I could wish that another man would come and take her. Not like you. Not my kind of a man. But some damned long-haired violin player that I couldn't touch for the fear of mashing him like a rotten apple. If a sneaking fool like that should come along and walk off with Kate Malone, Harrigan, I'd be a happy man, after a while. After the poison boiled down in me, I'd be a happy man."

The waiter came in, but not with a stack of dishes piled on his arm. Instead, he came with an armed man walking on each side of him, and behind this leading trio there moved others, a whole dozen or more of stalwarts.

Harrigan gave them one side-glance.

"They've come for us, Angus," he said.

"There's hardly a round dozen of 'em," answered MacTee, calmly. "And if they knew us, Danny—if they knew us as we know ourselves—wouldn't the fools bring the whole town together before they tried to come at the bare hands of Harrigan and MacTee?"

He who walked on the right hand of the waiter was built like a lumberjack and dressed like a lumberjack in a plain Mackinaw. On the lapel of the coat was a steel badge, brighter than silver.

He was such a big man that he did not touch a weapon, in making this arrest. He merely stepped to the table and rapped his brown knuckles on the top of it.

"Stand up, you bohunks," he said. "Hoss thieves get free board and room, in this here town of Yellow Gulch."

CHAPTER 7
The Men of Yellow Gulch

Harrigan looked at the deputy sheriff and at the fellows ranging beside him, and realized that they were men.

"All right," he said to MacTee, "I guess we'll have to stick up our hands, partner."

"We will," said MacTee, and rising to his feet, he brought up his fist like the head of an iron mace. It bashed the deputy sheriff under the jaw and sent him staggering across the floor. Harrigan selected the ex-sailor who had betrayed them. It was neither an uppercut nor a swing nor a straight punch that he used, but his favorite hook. The hook of Harrigan was like the snapping of a whip-lash. His blow struck the jaw of the waiter, and that unfortunate man fell on his hands and knees.

Then Harrigan and MacTee raised a frightful yell and charged home among the men of Yellow Gulch. Whoever they struck fell or staggered far away. That single charge should have ended the fight at once, for guns could not be used in the tangled heart of this melee.

But Harrigan saw a strange thing. The men of Yellow Gulch might be felled, but they would not stay down. The deputy sheriff, the first to drop, was already on his feet and coming straight into the thick of the fight. The ex-sailor was up, also, and charging. And all the other men of Yellow Gulch came in with cheerful shouts. Their eyes shone, and it was plain that they considered this a delightful game. Their bodies were of India rubber; their jaws were of whalebone; and their souls were the purest flame of battle.

Just as Harrigan finished these observations, two ponderous fists landed on his jaw from opposite sides. He dropped on his face.

When he wakened, a pair of monstrous legs bestrode him. It was MacTee, bellowing like a mad bull, striking right and left.

As Harrigan gathered his feet and hands under the weight of his body, the men of Yellow Gulch fell back a little, and the deputy sheriff stood before MacTee with a gun in either hand.

The deputy sheriff was no longer what he had been. The left side of his face was a great red puff. His right eye was closed. His coat was half ripped from his body.

"Stick up those hands, or I'll blow you to hell!" shouted the deputy sheriff.

But Harrigan dived along the floor, struck the legs from beneath the man of the law, and as the revolvers drilled eyeholes for the sunlight through the wall, Harrigan arose again into the fight.

"Harrigan!" thundered MacTee, a drunken joy in his voice, as he saw that his friend was again in the fight. "Harrigan!" he roared, as though it were a battle cry.

He caught up a chair and swung it.

"Harrigan!" he bellowed. "Harrigan!"

With each shout, he struck down a man. Half the little crowd of Yellow Gulch warriors were on the floor, and through the rest, Harrigan and MacTee charged to the side entrance to the dining room.

They heard an uproar of pursuit behind them. As Harrigan slammed and locked the door behind them, a bullet clipped through and split one panel. But the door held, nevertheless, while the two fugitives sprinted with lengthened legs down a narrow alley, and straight out of the little town of Yellow Gulch into the woods.

The green of the trees covered them. And presently they were sitting at the side of a little brook that wandered through the forest.

They smoked cigarettes, considered the brightness of the patches of the sun, and the brown of shadows upon pineneedles, and listened to the quiet conversation of the flowing water.

Finally MacTee announced: "We were licked and chucked out. We were chucked out with no breakfast, even. What's the matter with us, Harrigan? We used to rate as men. Now what are we?"

Harrigan shook his head. He was peeling off his clothes, and when he had finished that task, he stepped into the water of the brook and scrubbed from himself the signs of battle. At last he redressed and lay on the bank in the shadow.

"This Yellow Gulch," he observed, at the last, "is the sort of a town that we ought to know a whole lot more about, MacTee. It's full of folks that I could be glad to see, and so could you."

"I could," agreed MacTee. "It's a town worth having and a town worth knowing. Did you see that yellow-headed fellow with the straight left?"

"I did," said Harrigan, caressing his face. "And there was the short man with the big shoulders and the overarm swing. You remember him?"

"Ugh!" grunted MacTee. "I couldn't plant him with a solid sock. Did you cop him?"

"I just managed to hit him in the pit of the belly,

and as he dropped I was able to uppercut him, and when he straightened from that, I clouted him on the jaw."

"With a hook?" asked MacTee.

"With a hook," said Harrigan.

"Danny," said MacTee, dreamily, "there's times when I love you more than a brother. What did he look like when you last saw him? I sort of missed him in the last few minutes."

"He looked like an astronomer," said Harrigan, after a moment of thought. "He was lying on his back and he seemed to be studying the stars."

MacTee laughed, broodingly.

Harrigan said:

"Are we beaten, MacTee, or what do you say?"

"The mountains are up and against us," said MacTee.

"They are," agreed Harrigan. "But if we lose her now, we'll never find her."

"Now," said MacTee, "that they know the quality of us, they'll be shooting on sight. And these people, they wouldn't know how to miss!"

"They would not," agreed Harrigan.

"So what do *you* suggest?" asked MacTee.

"I suggest," said Harrigan, "that we draw straws to see who goes into Yellow Gulch after dark and tries his best to get on the track of her."

MacTee shuddered.

"Draw to see who goes back into Yellow Gulch?" he echoed.

"That's the idea," said Harrigan.

MacTee groaned.

"All right," said he. "Pick out some straws, and we'll see."

Harrigan picked two blades of grass. The short one he laid under his thumb projecting less than the long one. Then he changed his mind and laid them with their ends exactly even.

"The long man goes to Yellow Gulch," said Harrigan.

"Good," said MacTee, and straightway picked the shorter of the pair.

Harrigan stared, opening his palm to reveal the long one.

"Well," said Harrigan, "that's the way I'd rather have it."

"You're a brave man, Danny," said MacTee. "And when we're this far from Kate, I don't mind saying that you're as brave as any man in the world. But you wouldn't be telling me that you'd rather be going into Yellow Gulch than sitting out here in the woods, waiting for news?"

"I would, though," argued Harrigan. "If I sat here, and you went in, I'd go mad. For I'd see you finding Kate Malone, for yourself. And I'd see you talking to her, persuading, and lying, until you got her for yourself."

"She's not there at all, most likely," said MacTee.

"Maybe not," said Harrigan. "But I'll go fishing in Yellow Gulch for her as soon as it's dark—and I'll be a happy man to start on my way!"

CHAPTER 8
Harrigan Goes to Town

MacTee WENT TO THE EDGE OF THE WOODS WITH Harrigan, where he looked with his friend at the glitter of the town lights.

"You're a brave man, Harrigan," said he, "considering the sort of men they have in Yellow Gulch. Good-bye, and God bless you. If a thing happens wrong to you, I'll find the man that did it, and plant him alive!"

So Harrigan went like a thief into the town.

If MacTee dreaded the place and the strong-handed men of it, so did Harrigan. But in his heart there was the wild and eerie passion that led him toward the girl.

So he went on until, upon the dark of an alley, a kitchen door opened, a dull shaft of yellow lamplight fell upon Harrigan, and a woman's voice shouted: "It's Harrigan! It's Harrigan!"

Harrigan ran.

It was as though the woman had called to furious hornets, all in readiness inside of a nest. Out they poured, the men of Yellow Gulch, to follow him. Doors slammed. The heavy feet of men hit the ground.

He fled across the main street, a gorge of revealing light that brought a shower of bullets after him. One of them kissed the tip of his right ear.

He bounded like a deer into a silent byway. A tall board fence rose beside it. He leaped, caught the top rim, swung himself over, and started for the fence on the opposite side.

Then the imp of the perverse made him decide to trust to his luck—so he dropped into a nest of high grass and lay still. At the same time, a pursuer swung over the top of the fence like a pole-vaulter, and another and another followed him.

What manner of men were these in Yellow Gulch, when all of them seemed able to match the best that Harrigan could do? His heart grew small in him, with wonder, and he shook his head as he lay in the tall grass, murmuring: "I must be pretty far West!"

A dozen, he counted, crossed the yard, vaulted the fence on the farther side, and rushed away. Other footfalls stormed through the street. Then gunshots broke out, far away. The noise diminished, the shouting turned corners and was obscured.

After that, a quiet footfall drew near to Harrigan. Then the voice of a girl said: "I've got a sawed-off shotgun loaded with buckshot. I've got you covered, and I can't miss. Get up out of that, Harrigan!"

Harrigan got up, at once. With a sawed-off shotgun, no matter in what hands, argument is futile. He saw that the girl was small. He saw that the gun in her hands was real.

So he lifted his arms above his head. This was something for the world to read in newspapers and laugh at—how Harrigan was captured by a girl, by a child!

"March up there through that screen door into the kitchen," said the girl. "And if you try to jump one side or the other, I'll blow you out of your socks!"

If they had men in Yellow Gulch, they had women, also! Harrigan walked a chalk-line to the back verandah, up the steps, and through the screen door of the kitchen. He faced the stove, his arms still lifted over his head. The screen door creaked gently behind him.

"All right," said the girl. "You can turn around."

He turned. She was not more than sixteen. She had freckles across her nose. She was rather small. But her eyes were of the divine Irish blue.

"So you're Harrigan," said she.

"I'm a piece of him," said Harrigan.

"It's you that licked Jim Bingham, is it?" said the girl.

"Who's Jim Bingham?"

"You licked him, and you don't even know his name? He's my brother."

"I know him, then," said Harrigan. "He's short and wide and he knows how to box. He's got black hair and a pair of eyes in his head."

"I'm mighty glad you noticed him," said the girl.

"Molly!" groaned a voice at a distance of two or three rooms.

"Ay, Jim. Wait a minute."

She added: "He's lying in there with a couple of busted ribs. But you don't look so big. Not to me, you don't."

"I'm not so big," said Harrigan, gently.

"But you licked Jim," she said, grimly, bitterly.

"I had the weight and the reach on him," said Harrigan.

"You had ten or twelve huskies socking at you, too," she answered, shaking her head. "I thought the Binghams were the best, but I guess they're not. The Harrigans must be close to the top."

"I got in a lucky punch," said Harrigan.

"Harrigan," said the girl, "why do you and MacTee steal horses and chase around after a girl that doesn't want you?"

"Who says that?"

"There's talk around."

"The talk's wrong," said Harrigan. "She wants one of us. We want to find which one."

"Ah?" said the girl.

"Yes. She wants one of us."

"She's mighty pretty," said the girl. "I saw her. She's beautiful. She's good, too, and she's kind, and gentle, and wise, and brave, and everything."

"Yes. She's everything," agreed Harrigan. "I've known her for a long time. I've known her since she was a ringer for you."

"Since she was what? Are you trying to flatter me, Harrigan?"

"The truth is not flattering," answered Harrigan. "I remember her when she was a ringer for you. And I've been following her ever since."

"Never mind who she's a ringer for," said Molly Bingham, flushing. "But go on and tell me what makes you think she wants one of you?"

"She said so, one day."

"It was a long time ago, then," suggested the girl.

"Yes, it was a long time ago," agreed Harrigan, sighing.

"Suppose that she took MacTee," said the girl. "What would you do?"

"I'd murder the black Scotch heart of him," said Harrigan.

The girl started.

"I think you mean it," she answered. "And yet you and MacTee fight for each other like two brothers."

"He's the best man in the world," agreed Harrigan, "except where Kate Malone's concerned."

At this, the girl chuckled, softly.

"Molly!" called her brother, in angry impatience.

"Be still, Jimmy. I'm coming in a moment," answered the girl.

"How did you know me?" asked Harrigan.

"I saw the red of your hair," answered the girl. "And who else but a Harrigan or a MacTee would be leaping the fences around Yellow Gulch at this time of the night?"

"True," said Harrigan. "I hadn't thought about that."

"I'm going to call for help," said Molly Bingham.

"If you do," answered Harrigan, "they'll never take me alive."

"Well, then," she replied, "I'll give you a chance. I'll send you to where Kate Malone is staying. But I'll have a promise out of you, first."

"I'll promise you the clouds out of the sky," said Harrigan.

"Harrigan," said the girl, "she loves either you or MacTee, and neither of you can guess which one it is. And she doesn't dare to give herself to one of you for fear that the other will make mincemeat of the lucky man. But now I'm going to take your word of honor that you'll go to her, Harrigan, and swear on the Bible to her that if she loves MacTee you'll do him no harm, but you'll go far away. Will you promise me that?"

Harrigan looked up at the ceiling, then down into the face of the girl.

"Well—" he said.

"Or else I'll raise a yell that'll bring all of the town to this spot. It's a mean town, too, Harrigan. There's a dozen of its best men that are wearing bumps and breaks because of you and MacTee, and all their friends, and themselves, are achin' to have another go at you."

"It's true," said Harrigan. "It's a tough town. The toughest that ever I found in my days."

"Will you promise me?"

"If she says that it's MacTee, will I go way off and never do him a harm?" repeated Harrigan.

"Ay. Will you promise that?"

"Yes," groaned the hesitant Harrigan.

"Good," said the girl. "Give your hand on it." She held out hers.

Harrigan looked at the hand and sighed.

"Be a man, Harrigan," said the girl.

Gingerly he took her hand. He closed his eyes, and sighed.

"Here's my promise," sighed Harrigan, "and God help me. Where'll I find her?"

"I know where she is," said Molly Bingham. "Go out to the front corner of the garden. Wait there. I'll soon be coming."

Harrigan went out through the darkness of a trance and stood in the garden. Presently the front door opened and closed. The girl stood beside him.

"Come with me," she said.

Harrigan followed her down a lane, and across an alley, and up a barren, empty street until they came to a little house retired among trees.

"She's in there," said the girl. "Wouldn't you feel shame, Dan Harrigan, to be hounding a girl like her, and making the world talk? Wouldn't you feel shame?"

But she was laughing, softly, as she walked up the path before him to the house.

When they came to the trees, she said: "Wait here!"

He waited. She went on. She climbed the steps through a soft shaft of lamplight. She knocked at the front door, then opened it and went inside.

Harrigan heard nothing. The coldness of ice water welled up in him, covered his heart, rose as high as his throat. He felt dizzy, and weak.

At last the front door of the house opened. Two women came out. One of them sat down at the top of the steps, and he knew that this was Molly Bingham.

The other came with hesitant steps down the path. At last, she reached a full halt, turned, and beckoned. Molly Bingham instantly ran and joined her. They came on together. A dullness of lamplight passed over them, and Harrigan saw the face of Kate Malone. His dizziness increased. He wanted to run away, leaving all questions unasked and unanswered.

Then they were close. Kate Malone halted. The younger girl stamped on the gravel of the path.

"Come on to her, then, you great hulk!" she said.

Harrigan strode looming through the darkness. When he came to Kate Malone, he dropped to one knee, and felt that it was the weakness of his legs that compelled him.

She made a gesture toward him. He caught her hand. It was cold and trembling.

"Poor Danny!" she said. "Did the brutes hurt you badly?"

At that, a wild hope filled him.

"Fists couldn't be hurting me, Kate!" he exclaimed. "Nothing but a word from you could hurt me. That's what I've come to learn from you. Tell me, Kate, that you love MacTee, and I'll take myself from your way. I'll never bother Angus. You'll be free with him, and God give you both happiness. But tell me the truth of it. Do you love Angus MacTee?"

He listened, breathlessly. The pause was long. The moments of it stung him like poisoned daggers.

Then she answered in a broken voice: "Ay, Danny—I love him!"

CHAPTER 9
Baiting a Trap

THE HOPE SICKENED AND DIED IN HARRIGAN AS A GREEN twig withers and droops in flame.

After a while, he got up to his feet. He kept on rising, when he was erect. He kept on drawing himself straighter and straighter, drawing in deeper breaths, telling himself silently that he would not die, that men did not die of wounds that words could make.

Someone was weeping. Well, that was like Kate Malone. She could not endure giving pain, and she was an old friend and a dear one. Yes, Kate would weep over him. This made tears sting his own eyes, until suddenly he saw that it was the other girl who was crying heartily, stifling her sobs.

But Kate stood with her hands clasped in front of her, and her face lifted toward the stars. She reminded him of a picture he had seen somewhere, he could not remember where.

He said: "Well, Kate, I'm taking myself away. If I were man enough, I'd go out into the woods and tell Angus that he's the lucky one. But I couldn't trust myself that far. If I looked at the face of Black Angus, and thought of him calling you his wife—I'd likely go mad. But I've sworn an oath and given my hand on it—and now I'll take your word and leave you."

He held out his hand. The cold hand of Kate was laid in his.

"You blithering idiot!" gasped Molly Bingham. "I never knew a redheaded man to be such a fool. Kiss her good-bye—and then see!"

There was a melancholy stirring in the soul of Harrigan.

"We've been through great things, Kate," he said. "Will you kiss me good-bye?"

He put his left arm around her, gently. She had not stirred, but still looked past him at the upper night. She was like a stone.

"Oh, Dan Harrigan, you half-wit!" said Molly Bingham. "You swore that you'd leave her if she loved MacTee. But make her swear your own oath that she loves him. Make her swear that it's true she loves MacTee!"

"Almighty thunder!" groaned Harrigan.

His left arm was no longer gentle. It crushed Kate Malone to him.

"Swear it, by God, Kate, and I'll leave you. Swear that you love MacTee. For if you don't mean it with all your heart—if it's only a trick to get me and all the murdering trouble out of the way—! Swear that you love him, Kate. The saying of it won't do with me."

But Kate Malone began to sob.

And that baffled Harrigan. It made him more bewildered than ever.

"She's only a poor liar, after all," said Molly Bingham. "Kiss her, Dan Harrigan, and see what's left of her pretending. Kiss her—the silly baby!"

But Molly Bingham was herself crying, and talking through her tears. And Harrigan knew that in all the days of his life he never would understand women truly.

He leaned to touch his lips to the face of Kate Malone. Her head dropped weakly against the hollow of his shoulder.

"Kate!" he cried out in an ecstacy of revelation. "You're mine. You belong to me! It isn't MacTee that you care for."

"It's you, Danny," said the girl. "It's always been you. But I've never dared to show what I feel, for fear of Angus MacTee. What can we do now? He'll kill you, Dan, if he finds out the truth."

"God means it to come to a showdown between us," said Harrigan. "I've got to see MacTee, and face him, and have it out."

"No!" cried the girl. "You'd never come back to me alive!"

"I've got to tell him that I've found you," said Harrigan. "I came in for both of us to find your trail, Kate. We're partners, Angus and I. We'll keep on being partners—till he goes for my throat! There's no other honest way out of it."

"Would you be honest with the devil, Dan Harrigan?" asked Molly hotly. "Well, no matter what MacTee would do to a man, he'll never touch a girl. Let me know where to find him, and I'll take him the word that you've found Kate, and that you and she are away together. I don't have to tell what the direction is."

"I can't let you go out and face him," said Harrigan.

"It's the one way to live up to your partnership with him," said Molly, briskly. "If you talk to him, you know it'll be the death of both of you. Tell me where to find him."

"Tell her," said Kate Malone.

So Harrigan, hesitantly, uncertainly, gave the word to Molly of how she could pass through the

157

woods and come to the creek, and so to the camp of Black MacTee.

"I'll be on my way," said Molly. "Kate, do up your things. Get out of Yellow Gulch with Harrigan. Take the Dormer Pass and head straight for the railroad. You'll be out of the reach of MacTee before long! Go fast! You have your own horse, Kate. And in the shed behind my house there's a big bay gelding that belongs to nobody but me. You can take that horse, Dan Harrigan. Good-bye, Kate! Good-bye, Harrigan!"

"Wait!" exclaimed Kate Malone. "Stop her, Danny!"

Harrigan barred the way of Molly. At the touch of his hand, she was still, laughing and trembling with excitement.

"What am I to say to you, Molly, darling?" said Kate. "And what's Dan to say to you? We'll owe you everything!"

"I could teach Dan what to say to me," said Molly. "If I were a year or two older, I'd fight you for him, Kate. Dan, if you lose her somewhere in the mountains, come back and you can find me!"

She slipped away and was instantly lost in the darkness. She had given them the means of escaping, and now she was determined to assure their safety still further, so that no harm whatever could overtake them. . . .

Running as fast as any boy, she got to the house of the deputy sheriff. He sat on his front porch with a wet towel around his head and various swellings discoloring his face.

"Hullo, Dave," said the girl. "I've got news for you that'll make you open both eyes!"

"It'll be a month before I get both eyes wide open," said the deputy sheriff. He had the shamelessness of a man whose courage has been proved over and over. He sat up and took the towel from his face. "It's not mumps that I caught, but the Harrigan," he explained with a grin. "What's the good news, Molly?"

"The Harrigan's gone," said the girl.

"The devil he has. Where?"

"Through the Dormer Pass with Kate Malone, and if you lift a hand to follow 'em, Dave, you're not a right man."

"Listen to her," said Dave's wife, chuckling. "I suppose she loves the red man!"

"I do," said Molly. "Who wouldn't love a man that can beat Dave, here? And my own brother laid up with some broken ribs from the same fist! Of course, I love Red Harrigan. But there's a thing for you to do, still. You can catch Black MacTee."

"Ay," said the deputy sheriff. "He has a fist like an iron club. I'd like to put hands on MacTee, and irons on him, too."

"You'd better have the irons on him before you try your hands," said Molly. "Get some of your best men, Dave. There are plenty in Yellow Gulch that'd be glad to be in at the killing of MacTee or of Harrigan. You know that!"

"I know that," agreed Dave, "and I'll do it."

He stood up from his chair.

"You'll be running the whole county before long, Molly," said he. "You're running Yellow Gulch already."

"As soon as I outgrow freckles," said Molly. "I'm going to run for governor. You won't take after Harrigan, Dave?"

"No," said the deputy sheriff. "Not if you tell me to keep my hands off him. I wouldn't dare." He chuckled again. "But this MacTee. Where is he, Molly?"

"You cut across town till you come through the woods to the creek. Go up the creek till you find a sandbar with the creek spilling over the two ends of it. Black MacTee will be somewhere there. And go carefully, Dave. He's a tiger."

"I'll have five men with me," said the deputy sheriff, cheerfully. "I'd rather walk into the cave of a mother grizzly than into a place where that black Scotchman is hiding!"

CHAPTER 10
Pursuit

Black MacTee, sitting on a rock at the side of the water, trailed his left hand in the icy current. His heart was aching with desire for a smoke, but he dared not smoke for fear that even the easily dissipated smoke of a cigarette might reach inquisitive nostrils and bring danger.

So, as he sat there, he occupied his mind and quelled his nerves by submitting his flesh to the biting chill of the stream. He was so engaged when he heard a faint rustling sound. It was a very small sound. It might have been the rustling of leaves when branches toss slightly. It might have been the step of a wild beast inside the wood.

But the nerves of MacTee were drawn taut, and therefore he lifted his head to listen. What he heard next was hardly a sound at all. It was rather a vibration, a nothingness of tremor that ran through the ground. But it sent MacTee into cover with the speed of a slinking cat.

He crouched in the shadow, looking out savagely, tensely, around him.

After a time, he heard another mere whisper. It was close beside him, and now he could make out the silhouette of a man moving from behind the trunk of a tree, coming toward the sandbar.

MacTee reached out his arm, massive and rigid as the walking beam of a great engine. With the sharp, deadly knuckles of his second joints, he struck the stalking silhouette behind the ear. The sound was very muffled. It was not as loud as the noise a chopper makes when it is struck into soft meat. And yet the hunting figure relaxed, at once.

MacTee, taking a single long stride forward, caught the slumping body before it could crash to the ground.

With that burden in his arms, he straightened, and stalked away soundlessly.

On his left, he made out another dim form, slipping in the opposite direction, and he felt that he had been betrayed, and by Harrigan! The thought stopped his heart with cold sickness. There was no rage in him, at the moment. There was only that unutterable smallness of soul and despair as he thought that Red Dan Harrigan might have betrayed a partner.

He locked that misery behind his teeth and went on, stepping softly. When the burden he carried began to moan, faintly, and to stir in his arms, he was at a considerable distance from his starting point. So he put the man on his feet and shook him. Searching through his clothes, MacTee found a revolver and took it away from his captive.

"Who are you?" asked MacTee.

The other muttered: "Lord God, my head's smashed in!"

"It'll feel better, after a while," said MacTee. "What d'ye mean by sneaking through the night like a mountain lion hunting mutton? Who are you?"

"I'm deputy sheriff Dave—"

"Ah," said MacTee. "You're the deputy sheriff, eh?"

"I'm the deputy sheriff, and—"

"Somebody told you that you'd find me here?"

"Yes," admitted the man of the law, his wits still reeling from the blow that he had received.

"He told you, then!" muttered MacTee.

He drew in a long, long breath, to keep away the sense of stragulation.

"Even Harrigan!" said MacTee, miserably. "Anybody else—but not Harrigan a traitor! Traitors don't wear red hair!"

He added, aloud: "Where's Harrigan?"

"I don't know," said the deputy sheriff. "It's MacTee that has me? What happened?"

"What's happened doesn't matter, compared with what's *going* to happen pretty soon," said MacTee, "unless you tell me what's become of Harrigan. Have you caught him?"

"No."

"He's not in jail?"

"No, he's not in jail."

"Then where is he? D'you think I'll hesitate to squash your windpipe for you, unless you talk out to me, man?"

A shudder passed through the deputy sheriff. It was a tremor imparted to his body by the quivering of the angry hand of MacTee, as it gripped his throat. "Tell me or I'll shut your breath off!"

Dave was not one to betray a trust but he'd never been in a spot like this before. He felt the grip of MacTee begin to shut off his life.

"They're away together," he gasped, "him and Kate!"

"Him and Kate!" roared MacTee, a black mist swimming before his eyes. "Away? *Away?* Where?"

"Up the Dormer Pass, I reckon."

"Where's the Dormer Pass?" asked MacTee.

"There," said the frightened deputy, for he felt that he was in the hands of a madman: "There, to the right of that sugarloaf, in that cut, yonder. That's the Dormer. You can see the cloud rolling down through it."

MacTee looked, and he saw a white serpent of mist, brightened by the moon, crawling down the face of a mountain.

"The Judas!" groaned MacTee. "The damned, sneaking, Irish, blarney, hypocrite and traitor! He stole Kate and he sent the law after Angus MacTee to keep me from—"

"No," said the deputy sheriff. "He didn't send—"

"Be still, damn you!" snarled MacTee.

He dashed his fist into the battered face of Dave again, with such force that the deputy slumped senseless to the ground.

MacTee let him drop. Well ahead of him, through the trees, he could hear the shouting of several voices that blended and blurred together, and yet he could make out among them the calling of the name: "Dave!"

But there was something better close at hand. He could see the glint of the metalwork on bridles, the vague outlines of saddles, and one glistening spot of moonlight on the rump of a horse. Half a dozen of them were tethered in one group among the trees just before him.

"Dave! Dave!" yelled the searchers.

"Here!" groaned the feeble voice of the deputy.

MacTee stepped to the tethered mustangs, chose the biggest for himself, mounted it, untied the others of the group, and led them off at a quiet walk that turned into a jangling trot, and thence into a flying gallop that swept him straight toward the Dormer Pass.

CHAPTER 11
Flight

THE HORSES OF HARRIGAN AND KATE MALONE WERE already entering the thick mist. At once they were lost as though in smoke. Above them the strength of the moon pierced here and there through the gathering storm clouds. It peered as though through a window, and sent down a broad shaft of milky white, enabling the two riders to see one another, vaguely.

The way had grown extremely steep. The horses began to slip and slide. Even mountain horses, which are nearly as sure-footed as goats, could hardly negotiate those smooth rocks after the wet of the clouds had greased them.

They rode very close together, for a time. Then Harrigan dismounted. His great bulk made it difficult for his horse to climb. The girl, however, could still make better progress by remaining in the saddle.

It began to be difficult work. In half a dozen places, the horses could barely climb the sharp grades. They grunted. Their striking, sliding hoofs knocked long sparks out of the stones. And yet through this difficult time, they did not speak to one another. Not until Kate said, as they paused a moment, panting: "Do you think that we were right to take this pass?"

"Molly seems to be right about everything. She told us to take this one," answered Harrigan.

"Ay, but suppose that MacTee is able to make her talk to him, and gets the name of the pass out of her, and the fact that we've gone through, this way?"

"You don't know MacTee," said Harrigan. "He's man enough to smash a regiment, but he couldn't even whisper against a woman." He added, out of the largeness of his heart: "There's only one thing I regret, and that is that I didn't go find him myself before I left Yellow Gulch."

As he spoke, looking toward the girl, a radiance of moonlight flowed over her through the mist and made her like a form of glowing marble.

She said: "All right, Danny. We don't care, so long as we're here together, and safe for the minute. Only—"

"Only what?" urged Harrigan.

"It's too happy," she answered. "It can't last. There's a pricking in my blood that tells me. There's something that follows me like a ghost!"

They had come to a narrow point of the ravine, as she spoke, and here the wind, gathered as into a funnel, blew the mist rushing against their faces, then dispersed it as the wind gathers the dust of the desert and sweeps it off against the horizon.

They looked back to find that the pass was clear of mist, for the moment, behind them. And that was how they happened to see, far away, laboring up the slope of a very distant incline, the form of a horseman who looked larger than human, the horse driven frantic by constant spurring.

"MacTee!" said Harrigan.

He felt, in an instant, as though he were a small child followed by a demoniacal power. The very thought of MacTee became overpowering.

"Angus MacTee!" cried the girl. For even at that distance she, also, could recognize the bearing and size of the Black MacTee.

They looked at one another, silently. There was no longer a mist between them. They could see each other's face clearly, and as plainly as he could see the fear in the face of the girl, so she could see the fear in the face of Harrigan.

They fled up the pass, the hoofs of the horses striking out an iron clangoring.

Then the wind ceased. The clouds closed over them more darkly than ever. The moonlight ceased. They began to fumble forward through a wet, cold darkness.

Wind came again, but it did not clear away the clouds. It merely heaped on more and more mountainous vapors. Gusts of rain struck them wetly in the darkness. The hail came in great, pelting volleys of stones that dazed and hurt the horses. They whacked on the broad shoulders, they stung and cut the face of Harrigan, until he almost wondered that the girl could keep in her saddle.

But she made no complaint.

He dismounted again, went to her during a brief halt, and took her hands. They were as ice. He made her bend down from the saddle, and he kissed her face. It was icy, also. All her body was quivering. He knew that it was not the storm but the fear that was killing her, and he wanted to say words that would start the currents of her blood again. But he was not able to speak.

He went on, leading the two horses, with an ache of emptiness in his heart. He knew that he was afraid, and he feared lest she might despise him for the terror that he felt.

The storm increased. The wind came charging.

Under the weight of it and the sting of the hail and rain that charged it, the horses frequently halted and balked.

The moon shone through again briefly. Harrigan saw the mouth of a ravine that opened to the right, and into this he suddenly turned.

Now the high walls shut off the main torrent of the storm. The clouds flowed higher over them, and only occasional rattlings of hail beat against them. Then the hail ceased, and it rained, in torrents. The lightning sprang with it, making the mountainfaces above them fluctuate wildly.

It was by the lightning that he saw how the girl had bowed herself, clinging to the saddle pommel with both hands, her head down, as one who submissively endures, without hope.

He felt as though he had beaten her. He felt as though she were a child.

The next moment, they turned a narrow bend in the ravine, and the valley widened before them. The heavier roaring which he had thought to be the mere thundering of the wind he knew, now, to be the dashing of water. And on the edge of the canyon wall, he saw a small shack and shed, built together, of logs.

He made for that. It was a steep and treacherous slope that they had to cover to get to the cabin. It was so steep and covered with loose, rolling stones, that it seemed incredible that anyone should have built in such a spot. Something must have altered the place in the meantime. The slope must have increased with weathering, and the treacherous coating of loose stones, like so many ballbearings, must have rolled down from the upper part of the mountain.

They came to the cabin doorway, in which there was no door. A blare of lightning showed them that there was nothing but a bleak emptiness within the place.

They entered, and the regular pulsing of the lightning showed them the vacant hearth, three broken chairs and a loft of small poles overhead, with a ladder leading up to the attic trapdoor.

Harrigan climbed the ladder, tore down some of the poles, and came to the floor again. He broke up the poles and one of the chairs. Of the smallest fragments of the woods, he made a heap of tinder that had splintered off from the larger pieces. This he was able to light with his fourth match.

The yellow finger of flame took hold, mastered bit after bit of the refuse, burned up strong and clear. He built up the fire, cording the larger pieces around the flame.

Now the pale flare of the lightning was not the only illumination. There was, besides, the steadier, smokier light from the fire.

This showed to Harrigan the drooping figure of the girl. She stood close to the wall, one hand resting against it.

He went to her and touched her shoulder. She looked up to him. Her head fell back. She looked like one about to die.

"He could see the firelight," said Kate.

Harrigan studied her a moment. She was dripping wet, so that her clothes clung to her, and she looked amazingly helpless. It was not that he loved her less, but for the moment it seemed an amazing thing that two forces as great as Harrigan and MacTee should be engaged in mortal combat because of such a negligible thing.

Yet there was no question that she was worth more than the rest of the universe to both of them. They knew her of old.

But she was crushed and weak, now. She was not the independent, strong, and almost imperious creature she had been. Strength had gone from her with hope, and Harrigan knew why. It was because she felt that terrible events lay just around the corner from them.

Harrigan felt the same thing. It was a sense of inevitable and inescapable disaster.

"He would see the house, if he happens to turn down this ravine after us," said Harrigan. "But there's no reason why he should come this way. He'll go on through the pass, against the storm. That's the way of MacTee. He faces things. He fights them straight through. That's the greatness of him. Nothing turns him back. But if he happens to come through the ravine toward us, the lightning would show the cabin to him. The firelight won't matter."

"We'd better go on, then," said the girl, in a rapid, broken voice. "I don't want to stay here. It's like a cavern. I'd rather die in the open, than in a house—"

He put his hand against her face. It was burning hot. Despair ran through him in a sickening current.

Yet he made his voice calm to answer: "We'll have to stay here. As a matter of fact, there's no way of getting through without the danger of your catching pneumonia. I don't dare take you through this sort of weather."

"I won't melt," she said. She laughed a little, and repeated: "I won't melt."

It was like the voice of a child, trying to be brave. It was like the piping voice of a child. The heart of Harrigan was wrung by the sound of it.

"I'm taking the horses into the shed, the poor devils," he said to her. "You stay in here and take your clothes off. Take them off and wring them dry. Look at you. You're soggy. You're wet to the skin. Wring your clothes as dry as you can and drag them on again. I'll stay with the horses in the shed till I've fixed myself the same way."

She looked at him vaguely, as though she had not understood.

"Do you have to go away, Danny?" she said. "I don't want you to go away. Stay here with me!"

He was incredulous. He never had seen her so childish. Had the fever affected her mind? No, the dilation of her eyes gave the answer. It was not the heat of fever, but the intense cold of fear that had numbed her brain. Her lips were pale. Her eyes were as great as the eyes of an owl. He would hardly have recognized her face.

"Do what I tell you, Kate," he said, sternly. He talked like a father, to a child.

"Do what I tell you. Take off your clothes and wring them out. I'll be in the shed. Look. You tap on this partition, and I'll be back in here before even a lightning flash would be able to jump in and steal you away from me."

"All right," said the girl. "It's all right."

She was actually smiling, a crooked, wistful smile.

Harrigan mastered his heart and went outside. The rain blasted against his face. The roar of it was less than the sound inside the cabin, but every water drop cut at his skin.

The two horses were huddled against the wall of the house, shrinking from the sweep of the storm, and wincing from the strong glare of the lightning. Overhead, the thunder broke in an endless booming, like the water of a great cataract falling on a world of tin.

Harrigan pulled at the reins. The horses closed their eyes and stretched out their necks, without stirring, for a moment. Then they followed him to the shed.

No water entered it, and no wind. A musty smell of emptiness was there, and some of the warmth of the day that had not yet ebbed away.

Harrigan stripped off his clothes. He was glad

to give his strength to something. He almost tore the tough fabrics to pieces by the power with which he twisted them. Then he dragged them on again.

He took a bandanna, rolled it, and used that to rub down the horses until they were fairly dry. Their body heat set them steaming. By the lightning flashes he could see the steam rising. The rank smell of their damp pelts filled the little shed.

Suddenly the rain stopped beating. He looked out and discovered that the southern half of the sky was thronged with the great black forms of the storm, with lightning leaping beneath it. But in the northern portion of the sky there were enormous white waves of clouds, with the moon riding through them. It struck a solid bank, was lost in it, then burst through, flinging a luminous spray before it. Harrigan drew in his breath. The weight of the thunder, also, was withdrawn from his brain, as it were.

He hurried around to the front of the cabin. As he strode, the stones rolled suddenly under his weight. He was thrown flat, and skidded down the sharp incline until, at the very verge of the canyon, he found a finger hold, and stayed his fall.

From where he lay, he could look down a hundred yards of cliff that was almost sheer to where a river worked and whirled and leaped white in the bottom of the gorge.

He remained prone for an instant, waiting for his heart to stop racing. Then he got up, cautiously, and crawled to the cabin before he ventured to rise and go weak-kneed to the doorway.

Beside it, he called: "Kate!"

"Yes!" she answered.

"Are you through? May I come in?"

"Come in!" she replied.

He paused to look down the ravine. A wisp of mist was standing in it like a monstrous ghost.

Otherwise, it was empty, the moonlight glistening over the wet rocks.

Then he stepped inside and found the girl seated in a broken chair beside the fire. Her clothes were fitted to her skin as sleekly as the pelt of a wet animal. She had not followed his instructions. And she looked up at him with the same dumb, suffering eyes of fear!

CHAPTER 12
Fear

HE CROUCHED BESIDE HER. BENT IN THAT FASHION, HE felt far more keenly the hugeness of his bulk compared with her.

"What is it, Kate?" he asked.

She shook her head.

"It's MacTee," he insisted. "You're afraid of MacTee. You think that he's sure to come."

She closed her eyes.

"Well," said Harrigan, "you can't sit here in wet clothes. You'll have to do something about it. You'll have to wring them out, Kate. I told you that! Listen to me—if you won't do anything—if you just give up like a child—I'll have to undress you and wring out the clothes myself."

She opened her eyes and stared at him, as one who cannot understand.

He thought he would startle her into alertness. So he put out his hand and unfastened the top button of her khaki shirt. No change came in her uncomprehending eyes.

"Kate!" he exclaimed. "For God's sake, what's the matter!"

She closed her eyes again. The firelight touched her face, gently. The smoke, hardly drawn up the chimney at all from the hearth, curled behind her, and she was as the stuff of which dreams are made.

"It's MacTee," she answered. "Ever since the old days, I've been afraid, Danny. I've always known that a time would come when he and you would meet for the final time. I've always known, and now—"

"Now what?" asked Harrigan, staring in his turn—for the whole affair had grown ghostly.

She was silent. He touched her face. It was flushed and still burning hot. Her hands were hot, too, and dry. When she looked at him, there was a film over her eyes. A terrible feeling grew up in him that her brain was giving way under the strain.

"It's going to be all right," said Harrigan. "There's been enough to keep us apart. This is the last bad time—this night, the storm, and all of that. Afterwards, we're going to have plain sailing."

"Not on this earth!" whispered her lips.

A ghostly coldness stole through his blood. He wanted to ask her if she had the power of second sight.

She said, more loudly: "I know it's the end, Danny. I want to make the most of it. I want to be gay. I want to make you happy for the last time. But I can't. There's a shroud over me. I'm afraid. I'm buried alive in fear!"

"It's because you've been thinking of MacTee too long," said Harrigan. "You've made a ghost out of him. That's all. Besides, you're too excited. And it's night. The minute the sun comes up you'll forget all of this. Everything will be all right."

She lifted her head to answer, but instead of speaking, she stared with terrible eyes of fear past him, toward the door.

Then the heavy, booming voice of MacTee said: "Everything will be all right for her, Harrigan. But you or I will be dead!"

Harrigan rose to his feet slowly, like an old man whose joints are frozen by age.

He turned. And there in the doorway, filling it from top to bottom, stood MacTee. His clothes were glued to his body by the wet. The brim of his sombrero sagged heavily around his face. And the face itself was as Harrigan had seen it before, in times of settled passion, like gray iron. The storm had not affected him, any more than it could affect a steel beam.

"Come out!" said MacTee.

A revolver was held in his right hand, waist high. Harrigan studied it. He was far faster with a gun, far straighter in the shooting of it. Perhaps there was a ghost of a chance that he would be able to get out a weapon and end the thing with a bullet.

MacTee said: "Don't try it, Harrigan. Don't try it!"

And Harrigan knew that it would be folly to try. He looked back at the frozen face of the girl.

"Maybe this is the end, Kate," he said. "Maybe you've been seeing the future a lot more clearly than I can make it out."

He leaned and kissed her good-bye. Her face had been burning before. Now it was cold. She made no response. Harrigan was not in her eyes at all, but only the great body and the terrible face of MacTee.

Harrigan turned to the door and strode toward it. MacTee backed away from the entrance. Harrigan had stepped outside when the girl screamed, suddenly, a frightful sound, as though a bullet had torn through her flesh.

Harrigan glanced back. He saw that she had not risen from the chair. She simply sat as before, but with her head thrown back like a dying thing.

He stepped on into the night. The storm had retreated farther away.

It was so far away, now, that the voices in it could hardly be heard, and over the rest of the sky fled the shining white waves of clouds with the moon sweeping grandly through them.

MacTee still backed up, step by step. Harrigan followed him to a little distance from the hut. Then MacTee stopped and glanced around him, swiftly—very swiftly, for fear lest the least absence of care might enable the magic of Harrigan to produce a gun.

Then he said: "Hoist your hands, Harrigan!"

His voice had the clang of iron in it. Harrigan threw his hands well above his head. He knew that he was in touching distance, in breathing distance, of death.

"Turn your back to me!" commanded MacTee.

Harrigan turned his back. That was the hardest thing to do, to turn one's back on a nightmare terror. But he turned his back, little by little.

MacTee stepped up to him and laid the weighty muzzle of the revolver in the small of Harrigan's back.

"If you make a move—if you even breathe," said MacTee, "I'll blow your spine in two!"

"I won't move," said Harrigan.

The hand of MacTee searched him. It found two revolvers and threw them away. It found a knife, and threw it away.

The pressure of the gun was removed. MacTee drew back.

"Turn around again," he said.

Harrigan turned.

MacTee weighted the Colt in his hand.

"I ought to kill you like a dog," he said. "You went into Yellow Gulch to search for both of us. You found Kate. You told her enough lies to get her for yourself. Then you got hold of the deputy sheriff and told him where to find me. You're a traitor. You're a treacherous dog, and I ought to shoot you like a dog. But killing with a bullet wouldn't do me much good. I'm going to use my hands on you, Harrigan. I'm going to kill you with my hands."

He tossed the revolver away and spread out his great hands.

"It's been coming to you for a long time," said MacTee. "And now you're going to get it!"

"I didn't send the deputy sheriff," said Harrigan honestly. "I'm not such a sneak. I sent a girl to let you know—"

"My God," shouted MacTee, "are you going to try to lie out of it like a dirty dog? Are you going to turn yellow when the pinch comes!"

And as he spoke, he rushed in at Harrigan.

Harrigan struck with all his might. His fist glanced as on rock, but he was able to sidestep the rush.

He turned and met it again. After the first blow, his heart was working again.

"I'm going to tear you to bits!" said MacTee, wiping the blood from his face.

"MacTee," said Harrigan, "there never was a time when a Scotchman could beat an Irishman. It's the end of you, damn you! Come in and take it."

MacTee laughed. It was a terrible thing to watch and a terrible thing to hear, that laughter of MacTee. And he came in again, with a leap.

There was no stopping him. Harrigan knew it. He hammered in a long, overarm punch that landed solidly in the face. Then he doubled over quickly and got a low hold, straightened, and heaved the weight of MacTee over his shoulder.

The hand of MacTee gripped at him. With one gesture it tore coat and shirt from his back. Harrigan saw the white flash of the moon on his body. He looked down, and glimpsed the corrugated strength of his muscles, and laughed in turn. The battle-madness had entered him.

He ran in as MacTee arose, and shouted: "Now, MacTee! Now, Angus! We'll see who's the better man!"

So he plunged straight into the embrace of MacTee.

He had reason to regret it, the instant later. For the arms of MacTee were iron, hot iron, that shrank into place around Harrigan and crushed him. The power of a machine squeezed the breath from Harrigan.

In a sudden panic, he beat at the head and at the body of MacTee. He saw that it was as idle as splashing drops of water off a rock. His wind was almost gone. He tried for another grip by shooting his right arm under the armpit of MacTee and bending his forearm over the shoulder. By chance he fixed his grasp on the point of MacTee's jaw. The flesh was no more than a thin masking for the bone. It was against the bone that the grip of Harrigan was biting.

In the meantime, his own breath was gone. He jerked with all his might. The face of MacTee was convulsed to the mask of a beast, a dead beast, glaring with eyes of glass from the wall of a hunting lodge. The great neck muscles of MacTee bulged out to meet the strain. His whole body shook as Harrigan jerked with all his might, again and again, striving to bend back the erect head.

There was a sudden giving. The head of MacTee had gone back an inch, another inch. He groaned in an agony. They turned slowly. Bit by bit the head of MacTee was going back. His body began to bend at the waist. His knees sagged. He became smaller than Harrigan. He tottered. He was about to fall, but that was not enough for Harrigan, who suddenly shifted his clutch lower. The great spread of his fingers, like talons, fastened across the throat of MacTee.

That was the end. He held the life of the man. A bubbling, gasping sound came from MacTee's lips. He staggered this way, and that. It was a miracle that his stalwart legs still could hold him up, when he was dying on his feet.

Dying—all that was MacTee now pinching out in darkness; all the lion of courage and savage cruelty and greathearted friendship, also diminishing like a light that will fail and can never be kindled again.

"Angus!" groaned Harrigan. "I can't be murdering you, man!" He added: "Say that you've had enough—I can't be murdering you!"

But he knew, as he said this, that it was a vain appeal, for Black MacTee had never surrendered before, and he would never surrender now. How could that nature admit defeat?

Suddenly Harrigan loosened his grasp.

"I can't do it, MacTee!" he groaned, drawing back.

He had been in so close that there was no chance for those hammering bludgeons, the fists of MacTee, to strike a vital spot. But drawing away, he came into perfect range. At the last instant, he saw the danger coming like a shadow, from the corner of his eye. He tried to raise his left arm to block the punch. But his hasty guard was beaten down. A ponderous mass struck full and fair on the side of his chin, near the point. The shock was telegraphed into his brain like a thunderclap, while the darkness of thunderclouds spread over his eyes.

The moonlight seemed to disappear. Before him all was the thick of night.

In that murk of darkness, he saw a vague silhouette drifting. He put up his hands and stretched them out. But terrible blows struck him and knocked across his brain showers of fiery sparks. They gave him only light by which to see his own coming destruction. He was beaten, and he knew that he was beaten.

A wave of sick weakness came over him. He fell on hands and knees. The darkness, at the same time, cleared instantly from his mind, letting in the fullness of the moonlight, so that he could see the valley, the pale boat of the moon, the clouds that fled down the wind.

He saw MacTee, in the act of catching up a great, jagged stone, and heaving it into the air.

A sudden lightness of body and a strength of limb enabled Harrigan to rise. Once upon his feet, he could only stand there, tottering, his helpless arms hanging at his sides.

He saw the stone heaved back, until the strain of the effort was shown in the whole body of MacTee, prepared to deal the final stroke.

But MacTee did not strike. The stone dropped out of his hand and thumped its weight heavily against the ground.

"Damn you, Harrigan," said MacTee, "I can't do it. You're a traitor, Harrigan. But I can't finish you off the way you deserve to be finished!"

Harrigan pointed toward the cabin.

"It's the girl that counts, MacTee. She's half out of her mind with fear of you. We've got to show ourselves to her—alive!"

He stumbled forward. His knees were so uncertain that he was in danger of falling. MacTee gripped him by the arm and sustained him. They moved forward crookedly toward the cabin.

"Why did you do it, Harrigan?" asked MacTee.

"Why did you knife me in the back? Why did you tell 'em where to hunt me down?"

"I didn't," said Harrigan. "I'll swear on the Book, MacTee, that I left a girl behind to take the news to you that I was gone, and Kate with me. Maybe she was afraid to go and thought she'd do better by sending men and guns. I don't know. But I wouldn't stab you in the back, MacTee—as you've tried to stab me, many a time!"

"You lie," said MacTee.

He released the arm of Harrigan. And Red Harrigan, giving his head a shake, turned like a bull on MacTee.

"All down the railroad line, you left the railroad dicks ready to put lead in me. Answer me that, MacTee!"

"Are you going to bring up the past?" asked MacTee, gloomily. "Are you going to—"

A faintly murmuring voice broke in upon them from the cabin.

"Hush!" said MacTee. "Do you hear?"

They hurried into the cabin, and there they found that the girl was slumped against the wall of the shack, her head fallen on one shoulder, her eyes closed, her face crimsoned with more than the heat of the firelight.

MacTee put his hand on her forehead.

"She's burning with the fever, Danny!" gasped MacTee. "Ah, Harrigan, what have I done?"

Harrigan brushed him aside. It was not hard to do. There seemed to be no strength remaining in MacTee, for the moment. Harrigan pressed his face against her breast and heard the rapid hammering of her heart.

"It's the shock that's made her sick, Angus," he said. "And happiness will make her well, again. I'm sure of that. Make her know that we're friends."

"Friends?" said MacTee. "I'd rather be friends to a snake than to a Harrigan!"

"You fool!" said Harrigan. "Do you think that *I* want your friendship? I wouldn't have the whole man of you, not a dozen a nickel. But it's the girl that I'm thinking of. Make her know that you're not hounding the trail of her and me, now!"

MacTee stared sourly at the redheaded man. Then he leaned and called: "Kate! Kate Malone! Oh, Kate, do you hear me?"

She opened her eyes and looked uneasily toward him. Fear began to gather in her face.

"Hush, Kate," said MacTee. "Here's Dan Harrigan beside me. Do you see that? And we're friends, Kate. We'll be friends all the days of our life. There's nothing to be afraid of!"

She looked blankly at him.

"Is it true, Danny?" she said.

"It's true," said Harrigan.

"Then let me sleep again," said the girl. "I haven't slept, I haven't dared to rest, for years and years—"

"Oh, God," said MacTee. "What have I done, if she dies, Harrigan?"

"I'll tell you, MacTee," said Harrigan.

"Tell me, then," said Angus MacTee, "and curse me, Dan. Damn my heart black, because black it is!"

"You're talking like a fool, MacTee," said Harrigan. "What's in a man has to come out of him. You loved her too much to want to see her turned over to a man like me, that's all. I'm not worthy of her. Neither are you. God pity her for coming into the hands of either of us, Angus. But God knows you're a better man than I am. If there's a black devil in you, there's a red devil in me."

"You're raving, Danny," said MacTee. "It hurts me to see you make such a fool of yourself. Stay here with her. Hold her life in your hands like a young bird, and I'll be back with a doctor to take care of her for you."

Instantly he was gone through the door of the cabin. The galloping hoofs of his horse went ringing up the valley and faded away into nothingness.

CHAPTER 13
Out of the Shadows

It was a long, long night for Dan Harrigan. He climbed the rock to the wooded mountainside above and broke off evergreen branches until he had enough armloads of them to make a bed. He beat them dry, built them soft and thick in the cabin, near the fire, and spread a saddle blanket over them. There he put the girl.

She merely groaned in her sleep as he lifted her. Another saddle blanket covered her. Harrigan sat beside her and watched through the hours.

Her breathing grew easier and more regular, and deeper. Another light than the red of the fire began to enter the cabin, and turning his head, Harrigan saw the doorway brightened by the coming of the day.

A greater hope came up in Harrigan at the same time. He went to the door and stared out at the dawn, which was brightening the mountains above them.

"Dan!" called a voice behind him.

He whirled about and found her sitting up, braced on both arms.

"I've been dreaming," said the girl. "I thought that MacTee came!"

"Hush," said Harrigan. "He came, and he's gone again. He'll never trouble us again!"

He heard the clattering hoofs of horses coming down the valley, over the rocks. So he went to the doorway, and looking out, he saw three riders, of whom the first was MacTee.

As they came up, Harrigan saw that the other two were elderly men, frowning with grave thoughts and with the labor of their ride into the mountains. They dismounted.

"Two would be better than one, for what's wrong with Kate," said MacTee. "Here's Doctor Harden."

"She's better," said Harrigan to the doctor. "She's a lot better. I think the fever's dead in her."

The doctor gave him a rather biting glance, then entered the cabin. Harrigan remained outside with the other two.

"It's a strange business," said the other visitor, shaking his head. "What the law will say to this kidnapping in the middle of the night—what the law will say to that, you know as well as I do, Mr. MacTee."

"Let the law be damned," said MacTee. "There are things above the law, I can tell you. And one of them is Harrigan and MacTee, just now."

The voice of the doctor spoke from within.

"She wants to see both of you—Harrigan and MacTee."

They entered. Her face was half white and half flushed. Eagerly she fixed her glance upon MacTee.

"Is it true, Angus?" she asked. "Are you the friend of Dan Harrigan, now and always?"

MacTee scowled at Harrigan, but he nodded.

"Was there ever a man made for a better friend than Harrigan?" he said. "I'll tell you this, Kate. I came up last night to find him and murder him. We fought it out. He could have choked the life out of me, Kate. He had my life in the tips of his fingers, but he wouldn't take it. And then the chance came to me. I had him helpless, and I couldn't finish him. There's a charm on us, Kate. We can't harm one another. And if you want him, you want the better man of us."

"Take his hand, then, Angus," said the girl.

"Here, Danny," said MacTee.

He turned and gripped the ready hand of Harrigan.

"I wish to God that I'd never laid eyes on you, Dan," said MacTee. "But now that it's too late for such wishing, I hope to the same God that nothing will ever come between us again!"

"Why," said Harrigan. "Why, Angus, if we put our hands together, not even the devil could tear 'em apart. And there's my hand for life."

"Kiss me, Danny," said the girl. "God bless the two of you. This is the happiest day the world ever saw. Kiss me, Angus, too."

MacTee leaned over her.

"It's a way of kissing good-bye to what I've wanted the most in my life," said he. "But there you are, Kate." He touched his lips to her forehead. "I've kissed one part of you good-bye but not the friend in you, Kate."

"No," she said, with sudden tears running down her face. "Never that."

"Come in here, now," exclaimed MacTee, rising. "I brought two doctors, to make all well. I'm going to see an end of this damned business and get it off my mind for good. Come in here, Johnson."

The solemn face of the other stranger appeared in the doorway.

"Here's a sky-pilot," said MacTee. "He'll tie

your hand into the hand of Harrigan. I'm going outside till the trick's turned. Afterwards, I'm coming back inside to see what Mrs. Danny Harrigan looks like, and how she wears her new name!"

He strode out through the doorway.

"You must make him happier, Danny," said the girl. "Make him come back and be our witness. Can you lead him back in here?"

"Can I?" said Harrigan, joyously. "Why, I could lead him now with a silk thread. I could lift the whole weight of the soul of him on the tip of my little finger. For didn't you see, Kate? The blackness has gone out of MacTee forever!"